✔ KU-142-884

The Triumph of the Scarlet Pimpernel

1794, three years since the stirring events described in THE SCARLET PIMPERNEL. *Once again the Scarlet Pimpernel himself is caught up in the terrifying and extraordinary intrigues of the French Revolution. This time he is instrumental in bringing about the downfall of Robespierre himself, which was the beginning of the end of horror and brutality.*

Baroness Orczy

The Triumph of the
SCARLET
PIMPERNEL

 KNIGHT BOOKS

the paperback division of Brockhampton Press

ISBN 0 340 04137 4

This edition first published 1968 by Knight Books,
the paperback division of Brockhampton Press Ltd, Leicester
Second impression 1970

Printed and bound in Great Britain by
Cox & Wyman Ltd, London, Reading and Fakenham

First published by Hodder and Stoughton 1922
36 impressions

Contents

1 | 'The everlasting stars look down . . .'

NEARLY five years have gone by!

Five years, since the charred ruins of grim Bastille set the seal of victory upon the expression of a people's will and marked the beginning of that marvellous era of Liberty and of Fraternity which has led us step by step from the dethronement of a King, through the martyrdom of countless innocents, to the tyranny of an oligarchy more arbitrary, more relentless, above all more cruel, than any that the dictators of Rome or Stamboul ever dreamed of in their wildest thirst for power.

On this day of April 1794, year II of the New Calendar, eight thousand men, women, and not a few children, are crowding the prisons of Paris to overflowing. Four thousand heads have fallen under the guillotine in the past three months. All the great names of France, her noblesse, her magistracy, her clergy, members of past Parliaments, shining lights in the sciences, the arts, the universities, men of substance, poets, brain-workers, have been torn from their homes, their churches or their places of refuge, dragged before a travesty of justice, judged, condemned, and slaughtered; not singly, not individually, but in batches – whole families, complete hierarchies, entire households: one lot for the crime of being rich, another for being nobly born; some because of their religion, others because of professed free-thought. One man for devotion to his friend, another for perfidy; one for having spoken, another for having held his tongue, and another for no crime at all – just because of his family connections, his profession, or his ancestry.

For months it had been the innocents; but since then it has

7

also been the assassins. And the populace, still awaiting the
millennium, clamour for more victims and for more – for the
aristocrat and for the sans-culotte, and howl with execration
impartially at both.

But through this mad orgy of murder and of hatred, one
man survives, stands apart indeed, wielding a power which the
whole pack of infuriated wolves thirsting for his blood are too
cowardly to challenge. The Girondists and the Extremists
have fallen. Hébert, the idol of the mob, Danton its hero and
its mouthpiece, have been sent to the scaffold. But this one
man remains calm in the midst of every storm, absolute in his
will, indigent where others have grasped riches with both
hands, adored, almost deified, by a few, dreaded by all, sphinx-
like, invulnerable, sinister – Robespierre!

Robespierre at this time was at the height of his popularity
and of his power. The two great Committees of Public Safety
and of General Security were swayed by his desires, the Clubs
worshipped him, the Convention was packed with obedient
slaves to his every word.

Robespierre was in truth absolute master of France. The man
who had dared to drag his only rival down to the scaffold was
beyond the reach of any attack. By this final act of unparalleled
despotism he had revealed the secrets of his soul, shown himself to be rapacious as well as self-seeking. Something of his
aloofness, of his incorruptibility, had vanished, yielding to
that ever-present and towering ambition which hitherto none
had dared to suspect. But ambition is the one vice to which the
generality of mankind will always accord homage, and Robespierre, by gaining the victory over his one rival, had virtually
begun to rule, whilst his colleagues in the Convention, in the
Clubs and in the Committees, had tacitly agreed to obey. The
tyrant out of his vaulting ambition had brought forth the slaves.

Faint-hearted and servile, they brooded over their wrongs,
gazed with smouldering wrath on Danton's vacant seat in the

Convention, which no one cared to fill. But they did not murmur, hardly dared to plot, and gave assent to every decree, every measure, every suggestion promulgated by the dictator who held their lives in the hollow of his thin white hand; who with a word, a gesture, could send his enemy, his detractor, a mere critic of his actions, to the guillotine.

2 | *Feet of clay*

ON this 26th day of April, 1794, which in the newly constituted calendar is the 7th Floreal, year II of the Republic, three women and one man were assembled in a small, closely curtained room on the top floor of a house in the Rue de la Planchette, which is situated in a remote and dreary quarter of Paris. The man sat upon a chair which was raised on a dais. He was neatly, indeed immaculately, dressed, in dark cloth coat and tan breeches, with clean linen at throat and wrists, white stockings, and buckled shoes. His own hair was concealed under a mouse-coloured wig. He sat quite still, with one leg crossed over the other, and his thin, bony hands were clasped in front of him.

Behind the dais there was a heavy curtain which stretched right across the room, and in front of it, at opposite corners, two young girls, clad in grey, clinging draperies, sat upon their heels, with the palms of their hands resting flat upon their thighs. In the centre of the room a woman stood, gazing upwards at the ceiling, her arms folded across her breast. Her grey hair, lank and unruly, was partially hidden by an ample floating veil of an indefinite shade of grey, and from her meagre

shoulders and arms, her garment – it was hardly a gown –
descended in straight, heavy, shapeless folds. In front of her
was a small table, on it a large crystal globe, which rested on a
stand of black wood, exquisitely carved and inlaid with mother-
of-pearl, and beside it a small metal box.

Immediately above the old woman's head an oil lamp, the
flame of which was screened by a piece of crimson silk, shed
a feeble and lurid light upon the scene. The curtains in front
of the window, as well as the *portières* which masked both the
doors, were heavy and thick, excluding all light and most of
the outside air.

The old woman, with eyes fixed upon the ceiling, spoke in
a dull, even monotone.

'Citizen Robespierre, who is the Chosen of the Most High
hath deigned to enter the humble abode of his servant,' she
said. 'What is his pleasure today?'

'The shade of Danton pursues me,' Robespierre replied,
and his voice, too, sounded toneless, as if muffled by the heavily
weighted atmosphere. 'Can you not lay him to rest?'

The woman stretched out her arms.

'Blood!' she exclaimed in a weird, cadaverous wail. 'Blood
around thee and blood at thy feet! I see thee walking upon a
sea of blood, yet thy feet are as white as lilies and thy garments
are spotless as the driven snow. Avaunt,' she cried in sepulchral
tones, 'ye spirits of evil! Avaunt, ye vampires and ghouls! and
venture not with your noxious breath to disturb the serenity of
our Morning Star!'

The girls in front of the dais raised their arms above their
heads and echoed the old soothsayer's wails.

Now from a distant corner of the room, a small figure detached itself out of the murky shadows. It was the figure of a
young Negro, clad in white from head to foot. In the semi-
darkness the draperies which he wore were alone visible, and
the whites of his eyes. He carried a deep bowl fashioned of

chased copper, which he placed upon the table in front of the
old woman, immediately behind the crystal globe and the
small metal box. The seer then opened the box, took out a
pinch of something brown and powdery, and holding it between finger and thumb, she said solemnly:

'From out of the heart of France rises the incense of faith, of
hope, and of love!' and she dropped the powder into the bowl.
'May it prove acceptable to him who is her chosen Lord!'

A bluish flame shot up from out the depth of the vessel,
shed for the space of a second or two its ghostly light upon
the gaunt features of the old hag, the squat and grinning face
of the Negro, and toyed with will-o'-the-wisp-like fitfulness with the surrounding gloom. A sweet-scented smoke rose
upwards to the ceiling. Then the flame died down again, making the crimson darkness around appear by contrast more lurid
and more mysterious than before.

The old charlatan then repeated her incantations. Once more
she took powder from the box, threw some of it into the vessel
and spoke in a sepulchral voice:

'From out the heart of those who worship thee rises the
incense of their praise!'

A delicate white flame rose immediately out of the vessel.
It shed a momentary, unearthly brightness around, then as
speedily vanished again. And for the third time the witch
spoke the mystic words:

'From out the heart of an entire nation rises the incense of
perfect joy in thy triumph over thine enemies!'

All at once a bright red flame shot out of the bowl. Everything in the room became suffused with a crimson glow. The
old witch bending over her cauldron looked as if she were
smeared with blood, her eyes appeared bloodshot, her long
hooked nose cast a huge black shadow over her mouth, distorting the face into a hideous grin.

'Red! Red!' she lamented. She raised the crystal globe and

gazed fixedly into it. 'Always red,' she went on slowly. 'Thrice yesterday did I cast the spell in the name of Our Chosen ... thrice did the spirits cloak their identity in a blood-red flame ... red ... always red ... not only blood ... but danger ... danger of death through that which is red ...'

'A truce on riddles, Mother!' Robespierre exclaimed at last impatiently, and descended hastily from the dais. He approached the old necromancer, seized her by the arm, thrust his head in front of hers in an endeavour to see something which apparently was revealed to her in the crystal globe. 'What is it you see in there?' he queried harshly.

But she pushed him aside, gazed with rapt intentness into the globe.

'Red!' she murmured. 'Scarlet ... aye, scarlet! And now it takes shape ... Scarlet ... and it obscures the Chosen One ... the shape becomes more clear ... the Chosen One appears more dim ...'

Then she gave a piercing shriek.

'Beware! ... beware ... that which is Scarlet is shaped like a flower ... five petals, I see them distinctly ... and the Chosen One I see no more ...'

'Malediction!' the man exclaimed. 'What foolery is this?'

'No foolery,' the old charlatan resumed in a dull monotone. 'Thou didst consult the oracle, oh thou, who art the Chosen of the people of France! and the oracle has spoke. Beware of a scarlet flower! From that which is scarlet comes danger of death for thee!'

Whereat Robespierre tried to laugh.

'Someone has filled thy head, Mother,' he said in a voice which he vainly tried to steady, 'with tales of the mysterious Englishman who goes by the name of the Scarlet Pimpernel –'

'Thy mortal enemy, O Messenger of the Most High!' the old blasphemer broke in solemnly. 'In far-off fogbound England he hath sworn thy death. Beware –'

'If that is the only danger which threatens me –' the other began, striving to speak carelessly.

'The only one, and the greatest one,' the hag went on insistently. 'Despise it not because it seems small and remote.'

'I do not despise it; neither do I magnify it. A gnat is a nuisance, but not a danger.'

The woman once more raised the crystal globe to the level of her breast. Then she began to murmur.

'I see the Scarlet Flower quite plainly ... a small Scarlet Flower. ... And I see the great Light which is like an aureole, the Light of the Chosen One. It is of dazzling brightness – but over it the Scarlet Flower casts a Stygian shadow.'

'Ask them,' Robespierre broke in peremptorily, 'ask thy spirits how best I can overcome mine enemy.'

'I see something,' the witch went on in an even monotone, still gazing into the crystal globe, 'white and rose and tender ... is it a woman ...?'

'A woman?'

'She is tall, and she is beautiful ... a stranger in the land. ... Yes, it is a woman. ... She stands between the Light and that blood-red flower. She takes the flower in her hand ... she fondles it, raises it to her lips. ... Ah!' and the old seer gave a loud cry of triumph. 'She tosses it mangled and bleeding into the consuming Light. ... And now it lies faded, torn, crushed, and the Light grows in radiance and in brilliancy, and there is none now to dim its pristine glory –'

'But the woman? who is she?' the man broke in impatiently. 'What is her name?'

'The spirits speak no names,' the seer replied. 'Any woman would gladly be thy handmaid, O Elect of France! The spirits have spoken,' she concluded solemnly. 'Salvation will come to thee by the hand of a woman.'

'And mine enemy?' he insisted. 'Which of us two is in

danger of death now – now that I am warned – which of us
two? – mine English enemy, or I?'

Catherine Théot had remained rigidly still, in rapt contem-
plation. It seemed as if she pondered over the Chosen One's
last peremptory demand.

The next moment she took another pinch of powder out of
the metal box. As the seer dropped the powder into the metal
bowl, a highly scented smoke shot upwards and the interior
of the vessel was suffused with a golden glow. The smoke rose
in spirals.

The dictator of France felt a strange exultation running
through him, as with deep breaths he inhaled the potent fumes.
He was riding on a cloud. His throne was of gold. In his hand
he had a sceptre of flame, and beneath his feet lay, crushed and
mangled, a huge scarlet flower. The sybil's voice reached his
ears:

'Thus lie for ever crushed at the feet of the Chosen One,
those who have dared to defy his power!'

Then suddenly there came a sound, so strange and yet so
human, that the almighty dictator's wandering spirit was in an
instant hurled back to earth, brought down with a mighty jerk
which left him giddy, sick, with throat dry and burning eyes.

And yet that sound had been harmless enough: just a peal of
laughter, merry and inane – nothing more. It came faintly echo-
ing from beyond the heavy *portière*.

'What was that?' Robespierre murmured.

The old woman looked up.

'What was what, O Chosen One?' she asked.

'I heard a sound –' he mumbled. 'A laugh ... Is anyone
else in the room?'

She shrugged her shoulders.

'People are waiting in the antechamber,' she replied carelessly, 'until it is the pleasure of the Chosen One to go. As a rule
they wait patiently, and in silence. But one of them may have

laughed.' Then, as he made no further comment but still stood there silent, as if irresolute, she queried with a great show of deference: 'What is thy next pleasure, O thou who art beloved of the people of France?'

'Nothing . . . nothing!' he murmured. 'I'll go now.'

She turned straight to him and made him an elaborate obeisance, waving her arms about her. The two girls struck the ground with their foreheads. The Chosen One, in his innermost heart vaguely conscious of ridicule, frowned impatiently.

'Do not,' he said peremptorily, 'let anyone know that I have been here.'

'Only those who idolize thee –' she began.

'I know – I know,' he broke in more gently. 'But I have many enemies . . . and thou too art watched with malevolent eyes. . . . Let not our enemies make capital of our intercourse.'

The old hag almost prostrated herself before him, and clasping her wrinkled hands together, she said in tones of reverential entreaty:

'In the name of thyself, of France, of the entire world, I adjure thee to lend ear to what the spirits have revealed this day. Beware the danger that comes to thee from the scarlet flower. Set thy almighty mind to compass its direction. Do not disdain a woman's help, since the spirits have proclaimed that through a woman thou shalt be saved. Remember! Remember!'

Without another word he turned to go. The young Negro brought him his hat and cloak. The latter he wrapped closely round his shoulders, his hat he pulled down well over his eyes. Thus muffled and, he hoped, unrecognizable, he passed with firm tread out of the room.

For a while the old witch waited, straining her ears to catch the last sound of those retreating footsteps; then, with a curt word and an impatient clapping of her hands, she dismissed her attendants.

Again the old woman waited silent and motionless until that merry sound too gradually subsided. Then she went across the room to the dais, and drew aside the curtain which hung behind it.

'Citizen Chauvelin!' she called peremptorily.

A small figure of a man stepped out from the gloom. He was dressed in black, his hair, of a nondescript blonde shade, and his crumpled linen alone told light in the general sombreness of his appearance.

'Well?' he retorted dryly.

'Are you satisfied?' the old woman went on with eager impatience. 'You heard what I said?'

'Yes, I heard,' he replied. 'Think you he will act on it?'

'I am certain of it.'

'But why not have named Theresia Cabarrus? Then, at least, I would have been sure –'

'He might have recoiled at an actual name,' the woman replied, 'suspected me of connivance. The Chosen of the people of France is shrewd as well as distrustful. And I have my reputation to consider. But remember what I said: "tall, dark, beautiful, a stranger in this land!" so, if indeed you require the help of the Spaniard –'

'Indeed I do!' he rejoined earnestly. And, as if speaking to his own inward self, 'Theresia Cabarrus is the only woman I know who can really help me.'

'But you cannot force her consent, citizen Chauvelin,' the sybil insisted.

The eyes of citizen Chauvelin lit up suddenly with a flash of that old fire of long ago, when he was powerful enough to compel the consent or the co-operation of any man, woman or child on whom he had deigned to cast an appraising glance.

'My friends who are few,' he said, with a quick sigh of impatience; 'and mine enemies, who are without number, will readily share your conviction, Mother, that citizen Chauvelin can compel no one to do his bidding these days. Least of all the affianced wife of powerful Tallien.'

'Well, then,' the sybil argued, 'how think you that –'

'I only hope, Mother,' Chauvelin broke in suavely, 'that after your seance today, citizen Robespierre himself will see to it that Theresia Cabarrus gives me the help I need.'

Catherine Théot shrugged her shoulders.

'Oh!' she cried dryly, 'the Cabarrus knows no law save that of her caprice. And as Tallien's fiancée she is almost immune.'

'Almost, but not quite! Tallien is powerful, but so was Danton.'

'But Tallien is prudent, which Danton was not.'

'Tallien is also a coward; and easily led like a lamb, with a halter. He came back from Bordeaux tied to the apron-strings of the fair Spaniard. He should have spread fire and terror in the region; but at her bidding he dispensed justice and even mercy instead.'

'Well, then, if you are satisfied . . .' the old woman said.

'I am. Quite,' he replied, and at once plunged his hand in the breast-pocket of his coat. He had caught the look of avarice and of greed which had glittered in the old hag's eyes. From his pocket he drew a bundle of notes, for which Catherine immediately stretched out a grasping hand. But before giving her the money, he added a stern warning.

'Silence, remember! And, above all, discretion!'

'You may rely on me, citizen,' the sybil replied.

He did not place the notes in her hand, but threw them down on the table with a gesture of contempt. But Catherine Théot cared nothing for his contempt. She coolly picked up the notes and hid them in the folds of her voluminous draperies. Then as Chauvelin, without another word, had turned unceremoniously to go, she placed a bony hand upon his arm.

'And I can rely on you, citizen,' she insisted firmly, 'that when the Scarlet Pimpernel is duly captured . . .'

'There will be ten thousand livres for you,' he broke in impatiently, 'if my scheme with Theresia Cabarrus is success-ful. I never go back on my word.'

'And I'll not go back on mine,' she concluded dryly. 'We are dependent on one another, citizen Chauvelin. You want to capture the English spy, and I want ten thousand livres. So you may leave the matter to me, my friend. I'll not allow the great Robespierre to rest till he has compelled Theresia Cabarrus to do your bidding. Then you may use her as you think best. That gang of English spies must be found, and crushed. We cannot have the Chosen of the Most High threat-ened by such vermin. Ten thousand livres, you say?' the sybil went on, and once again, as in the presence of the dictator, a mystic exultation appeared to possess her soul.

But Chauvelin was obviously in no mood to listen to the old hag, and while with arms uplifted she once more worked her-self up to a hysterical burst of enthusiasm for the blood-thirsty monster whom she worshipped, he shook himself free from her grasp and slipped out of the room.

3 | *The fellowship of grief*

IN the antechamber of Catherine Théot's abode of mysteries some two hours later, half a dozen persons were sitting. The room was long, narrow and bare. Benches were ranged against the walls; the one window at the end was shuttered so as to exclude all daylight, and from the ceiling there hung a broken-down wrought-iron chandelier, wherein a couple of lighted tallow candles were set.

These persons who sat or sprawled upon the benches did not speak to one another. One or two of them were seemingly asleep; others, from time to time, would rouse themselves from their apathy, look with dim, inquiring eyes in the direction of a heavy *portière* which hung in front of a door near the far end of the room, and would strain their ears to listen. Now and then somebody would sigh, and at one time one of the sleepers snored.

Far away a church clock struck six.

A few minutes later, the *portière* was lifted, and a girl came into the room. She held a shawl, very much the worse for wear, tightly wrapped around her meagre shoulders, and from beneath her rough woollen skirt her small feet appeared clad in well-worn shoes and darned worsted stockings. Her hair, which was fair and soft, was partially hidden under a white muslin cap, and as she walked with a brisk step across the room, she looked neither to right nor left. Her large grey eyes were brimming over with tears.

Only one of the men, a huge, ungainly giant, whose long limbs appeared to stretch half across the bare wooden floor, looked up lazily as she passed.

A few more minutes went by, then the door behind the *portière* was opened and a voice spoke the word, 'Enter!'

There was a faint stir among those who waited. A woman rose from her seat, said dully: 'My turn, I think?' and, gliding across the room like some bodiless spectre, she presently vanished behind the *portière*.

'Are you going to the Fraternal Supper tonight, citizen Langlois?' the giant said, after the woman had gone.

'Not I!' Langlois replied. 'I must speak with Mother Théot. My wife made me promise. She is too ill to come herself, and the poor unfortunate believes in the Théot's incantations.'

'Come out and get some fresh air, then,' the other rejoined.
'It is stifling in here!'

It was indeed stuffy in the dark, smoke-laden room. The
man put his bony hand up to his chest, as if to quell a spasm
of pain. A horrible, rasping cough shook his big body and
brought a sweat to his brow. Langlois waited patiently until
the spasm was over, then, with the indifference peculiar to these
turbulent times, he said lightly:

'I would just as soon sit here as wear out shoe-leather on
the cobble-stones of this God-forsaken hole. And I don't want
to miss my turn with Mother Théot.'

'You'll have another four hours maybe to wait in this filthy
atmosphere.'

'What an aristo you are, citizen Rateau! the other retorted
dryly. 'Always talking about atmosphere!'

'So would you, if you had only one lung wherewith to inhale
this filth,' growled the giant through a wheeze.

'Then don't wait for me, my friend,' Langlois concluded with
a careless shrug of his narrow shoulders. 'And, if you don't
mind missing your turn . . .'

'I do not,' was Rateau's curt reply. 'I would as soon be last
as not. But I'll come back presently. I am the third from now.
If I'm not back you can have my turn, and I'll follow you in.
But I can't –'

His next words were smothered in a terrible fit of coughing, as he struggled to his feet. His heavy footsteps were heard
descending the stone stairs with a shuffling sound, and the
clatter of his wooden shoes. The women once more settled
themselves against the dank walls, with feet stretched out
before them and arms folded over their breasts, and prepared
once more to go to sleep.

In the meanwhile, the girl who, with tear-filled eyes, had
come out of the inner room in Mother Théot's apartments,

had, after a slow descent down the stone stairs, at last reached the open air.

The Rue de la Planchette is only a street in name, for the houses in it are few and far between. One side of it is taken up for the major portion of its length by the dry moat which at this point forms the boundary of the Arsenal and of the military ground around the Bastille. The house wherein lodged Mother Théot is one of a small group situated behind the Bastille, the grim ruins of which can be distinctly seen from the upper windows. Immediately facing those houses is the Porte St. Antoine, through which the wayfarer in this remote quarter of Paris has to pass in order to reach the more populous parts of the great city.

The girl who had just come out of the heavy, fetid atmosphere of Mother Théot's lodgings stood for a while quite still, drinking in the balmy spring air. For a minute or two she stood there, then walked deliberately in the direction of the Porte St. Antoine.

She was very tired, for she had come to the Rue de la Planchette on foot all the way from the small apartment in the St. Germain quarter, where she lodged with her mother and sister and a young brother; she had become weary and jaded by sitting for hours on a hard wooden bench, waiting her turn to speak with Mother Théot, and then standing for what seemed an eternity of time in the presence of the soothsayer, who had further harassed her nerves by weird prophecies and mystic incantations.

But for the nonce weariness was forgotten. Régine de Serval was going to meet the man she loved, at a trysting-place which they had marked as their own: the porch of the church of Petit St. Antoine.

Bertrand had agreed to meet her at five o'clock. It was now close on half past six. Régine had crossed the Rue des Balais, and the church porch of Petit St. Antoine was but a few paces farther on, when she became conscious of heavy, dragging foot-steps some little way behind her. Immediately afterwards, the distressing sound of a racking cough reached her ears, followed by heart-rending groans as of a human creature in grievous bodily pain. The girl, not in the least frightened, instinctively turned to look, and was moved to pity on seeing a man leaning against the wall of a house, in a state bordering on collapse, his hands convulsively grasping his chest. Régine unhesitatingly recrossed the road, approached the sufferer, and in a gentle voice asked him if she could be of any assistance to him in his distress.

'A little water,' he gasped, 'for mercy's sake!'

Just for a second or two she looked about her, doubtful as to what to do, hoping perhaps to catch sight of Bertrand, if he had not given up all hope of meeting her. The next, she stepped boldly through the wicket-gate of the nearest *porte-cochère*. A jug of water was handed to her by a sympathetic concierge, and with it she went back to complete her simple act of mercy.

For a moment she was puzzled, not seeing the poor vaga-bond there, where she had left him, half-swooning against the wall. But soon she spied him, in the very act of turning under the little church porch of Petit St. Antoine, the hallowed spot of her frequent meetings with Bertrand.

He seemed to have crawled there for shelter, and there he collapsed upon the wooden bench, in the most remote angle of the porch. Of Bertrand there was not a sign.

Régine was soon by the side of the unfortunate. She held up the jug of water to his quaking lips, and he drank eagerly. She sat down beside him, suddenly conscious of fatigue. He seemed harmless enough, and after a while began to tell her of his trouble. This awful asthma, which he had contracted in the campaign against the English in Holland, where he and his comrades had to march in snow and ice, often shoeless and with nothing but bass mats around their shoulders. He had but lately been discharged from the army as totally unfit, and as he had no money wherewith to pay a doctor, he would no doubt have been dead by now but that a comrade had spoken to him of Mother Théot, a marvellous sorceress, who knew the art of drugs and simples, and could cure all ailments of the body by the mere laying on of hands.

'Ah, yes,' the girl sighed involuntarily, 'of the body!'

'Ay!' he was saying, in response to her lament, 'and of the mind, too. I had a comrade whose sweetheart was false to him while he was fighting for his country. Mother Théot gave him a potion which he administered to the faithless one, and she returned to him as full of ardour as ever before.'

'I have no faith in potions,' the girl said.

'No more have I,' the giant assented carelessly. 'But if my sweetheart was false to me I know what I would do.'

'What would you do, citizen?' she queried gently.

'Just take her away, out of the reach of temptation,' he replied sententiously. 'I should say, "This must stop," and "You come away with me, ma mie!" '

'Ah!' she retorted impulsively, 'it is easy to talk. A man can do so much. What can a woman do?'

But he appeared not to have heard. Nor did he meet her terrified gaze.

'What did you say, citoyenne?' he murmured fretfully. 'Are you dreaming? . . . or what? . . .'

'Yes – yes!' she murmured vaguely, her heart still beating with that sudden fright. 'I must have been dreaming. . . . But you . . . you are better—?'

'Better? Perhaps,' he replied, with a hoarse laugh. 'I might even be able to crawl home.'

'Do you live very far?' she asked.

'No. Just by the Rue de l'Anier.'

He made no attempt to thank her for her gentle ministration, and she thought how ungainly he looked – almost repellent – sprawling right across the porch, with his long legs stretched out before him and his hands buried in the pockets of his breeches. Nevertheless, he looked so helpless and so pitiable that the girl's kind heart was again stirred with compassion, and when presently he struggled with difficulty to his feet, she said impulsively:

'The Rue de l'Anier is on my way. If you will wait, I'll return the jug to the kind concierge who let me have it and I'll walk with you. You really ought not to be about the street alone.'

'Oh, I am better now,' he muttered, in the same ungracious way. 'You had best leave me alone. I am not a suitable gallant for a pretty wench like you.'

But already the girl had tripped away with the jug, and returned two minutes later to find that the curious creature had already started on his way and was fifty yards and more farther up the street by now. She shrugged her shoulders, feeling mortified at his ingratitude, and not a little ashamed that she had forced her compassion where it was so obviously unwelcome.

4 | *One dram of joy must have a pound of care*

SHE stood, gazing on the retreating figure of the asthmatic giant. The next moment she heard her name spoken, and turned quickly with a little cry of joy.

'Régine!'

A young man was hurrying towards her, was soon by her side and took her hand.

'I have been waiting,' he said reproachfully, 'for more than an hour.'

In the twilight his face appeared pinched and pale, with dark, deep-sunken eyes. He wore cloth clothes that were very much the worse for wear, and boots that were down at heel. A battered tricorne hat was pushed back from his high forehead, exposing the veined temples with the line of brown hair, and the arched, intellectual brows that proclaimed the enthusiast rather than the man of action.

'I am sorry, Bertrand,' the girl said simply. 'But I had to wait such a long time at Mother Théot's, and –'

'But what were you doing now?' he queried with an impatient frown. 'I saw you from a distance. You came out of yonder house, and then stood here like one bewildered. You did not hear when first I called.'

'I have had quite a funny adventure,' Régine exclaimed; 'and I am very tired. Sit down with me, Bertrand, for a moment. I'll tell you all about it.'

'It is too late –' he began, and the frown of impatience deepened upon his brow. Already, without waiting for his consent, she had turned into the little porch, and Bertrand perforce had to follow her.

The darkness lent an air of solitude and of security to this tiny refuge, and Régine drew a happy little sigh as she walked deliberately to its farthermost recess and sat down on the wooden bench in its extreme and darkest angle.

Behind her, the heavy oaken door of the church was closed. The stone walls themselves appeared cut off from the world, as if ostracized. But between them Régine felt safe, and when Bertrand Moncrif somewhat reluctantly sat down beside her, she also felt almost happy.

He took her hand, obviously making an effort to be patient

and to be kind; and she, not noticing the effort of his absorption, began to tell him about her little adventure with the asthmatic giant.

'Such a droll creature,' she explained. 'He would have frightened me but for that awful churchyard cough.'

But the matter did not seem to interest Bertrand very' much; and presently he took advantage of a pause in her narrative to ask abruptly:

'And Mother Théot, what had she to say?'

Régine gave a shudder.

'She foretells danger for us all,' she said.

'The old charlatan!' he retorted with a shrug of the shoulders. 'As if everyone was not in danger these days!'

'She gave me a powder,' Régine went on simply, 'which she thinks will calm Joséphine's nerves.'

'And that is folly,' he broke in harshly. 'We do not want Joséphine's nerves to be calmed.'

'Bertrand,' she said firmly, 'you are doing a great wrong by dragging the child into your schemes. Joséphine is too young to be used as a tool by a pack of thoughtless enthusiasts.'

A bitter, scornful laugh from Bertrand broke in on her vehemence.

'Thoughtless enthusiasts!' he exclaimed roughly. 'Is that how you call us, Régine? My God! where is your loyalty, your devotion? Do you no longer worship God or reverence your King?'

'In heaven's name, Bertrand, take care!' she whispered hoarsely, and she looked about her as if the stone walls of the porch had ears and eyes fixed upon the man she loved.

'Take care!' he rejoined bitterly. 'Yes! that is your creed now. Caution! Circumspection! You fear –'

'For you,' she broke in reproachfully; 'for Joséphine; for Maman; for Jacques – not for myself, God knows!'

'We must all take risks, Régine,' he retorted more composedly. 'We must all risk our miserable lives in order to

end this awful, revolting tyranny. We must have a wider out-
look, think not only of ourselves, of those immediately round
us, but of France, of humanity, of the entire world.'

'And what are you? My God!' she cried passionately. 'You
and your friends, my poor young sister, my foolish little
brother? What are you, that you think you can stem the torrent
of this stupendous Revolution?'

'It is the still small voice,' Bertrand replied, 'that is heard
by its persistence even above the fury of thousands in full cry.
Our aim is to take every opportunity by quick, short speeches,
by mixing with the crowd and putting in a word here and
there, to make propaganda against the fiend Robespierre. One
day, one of us – it may be the humblest, the weakest, the
youngest; it may be Joséphine or Jacques; I pray God it may
be me – but one of us will find the word and speak it at the
right time, and the people will follow us and turn against that
execrable monster and hurl him from his throne, down into
Gehenna.'

'I know, I know, Bertrand,' she rejoined. 'Your aims are
splendid. You are wonderful, all of you. But Joséphine is so
young, so hot-headed! What help can she give you? And
Jacques! He is just an irresponsible boy! Think, Bertrand, think!
If anything were to happen to these children, it will kill
Maman.'

He gave a shrug of the shoulders and smothered a weary sigh.

'You and I will never understand one another, Régine,' he
began; then added quickly, 'over these matters.' He went on,
more quietly, 'In a great cause the sufferings of individuals
are nought beside the glorious achievement that is in view.'

'The sufferings of individuals,' she murmured. 'In truth 'tis
but little heed you pay, Bertrand, to my sufferings these days.'
She paused awhile, then added under her breath: 'Since first
you met Theresia Cabarrus, three months ago, you have eyes
and ears only for her.'

He smothered an angry exclamation.

'It is useless, Régine –' he began.

'I know,' she broke in quietly. 'Theresia Cabarrus is beautiful; she has charm, wit, power – all things which I do not possess.'

'She has fearlessness and a heart of gold,' Bertrand rejoined. 'Do you not know of the marvellous influence which she exercised over that fiend Tallien, down in Bordeaux? He went there ready for a wholesale butchery of all the royalists, the aristocrats, the bourgeois, over there – all those, in fact, whom he chose to believe were conspiring against this hideous Revolution. Well! under Theresia's influence he actually modified his views and became so lenient that he was recalled. You know, or should know, Régine,' the young man added in a tone of bitter reproach, 'that Theresia is as good as she is beautiful.'

'I do know that, Bertrand,' the girl rejoined with an effort. 'Only –'

'Only what?' he queried roughly.

'I do not trust her . . . that is all. Your infatuation blinds you, Bertrand, or you – an enthusiastic royalist, an ardent loyalist – would not place your trust in an avowed Republican. Theresia Cabarrus may be kind-hearted – I don't deny it. She may have done and she may be all that you say; but she stands for the negation of every one of your ideals, for the destruction of what you exalt, the glorification of the principles of this execrable Revolution.'

'Jealousy blinds you Régine,' he retorted moodily.

'No, it is not jealousy, Bertrand – not common, vulgar jealousy – that prompts me to warn you, before it is too late. Remember,' she added solemnly, 'that you have not only yourself to think of, but that you are accountable to God and to me for the innocent lives of Joséphine and of Jacques. By confiding in that Spanish woman –'

'Now you are insulting her,' he broke in mercilessly. 'Making her out to be a spy.'

'What else is she?' the girl riposted vehemently. 'You know that she is affianced to Tallien, whose influence and whose cruelty are second only to those of Robespierre. You know it, Bertrand!' she insisted, seeing that at last she had silenced him and that he sat beside her, sullen and obstinate.

There was silence after that for a while in the narrow porch, where two hearts once united were filled now with bitterness, one against the other. The girl shivered as with cold and drew her tattered shawl more closely round her shoulders. Goaded into saying more than she had ever meant to, she felt the finality of what she had said.

'Oh, Mother of God, have mercy!' she murmured through her tears.

Bertrand, shamed and confused, his heart stirred by the misery of this girl whom he had so dearly loved, his nerves strained beyond endurance through the many mad schemes which his enthusiasm was for ever evolving, felt like a creature on the rack, torn between compunction and remorse on the one hand and irresistible passion on the other.

'Régine,' he pleaded, 'forgive me! I am a brute, I know – a brute to you, who have been the kindest little friend a man could possibly hope for. Oh, my dear,' he added pitiably, 'if you would only understand . . .'

'I do understand, Bertrand,' she said gently. 'And you must never ask my forgiveness, for you and I have loved one another too well to bear anger or grudge one toward the other. It is getting late, and Maman will be anxious. Another time we must have a more quiet talk about our future. But,' she added, with renewed seriousness, 'if I concede you Theresia Cabarrus without another murmur, you must give me back Joséphine and Jacques. If – if I – am to lose you – I could not bear to lose them as well. They are so young . . .'

'Who talks of losing them?' he broke in. 'And what have I to do with it all? Joséphine and Jacques are members of the Club. They may be young, but they are old enough to know the value of an oath. They are pledged just as I am, just as we all are. I could not, even if I would, make them false to their oath.' Then, as she made no reply, he leaned over to her, took her hands in his, tried to read her inscrutable face through the shadows of night. 'You would not have them false to their oath?' he insisted.

She made no reply to that, only queried dully:

'What are you going to do tonight?'

'Tonight,' he said with passionate earnestness, 'we are going to let hell loose around the name of Robespierre.'

'Where?'

'At the open-air supper in the Rue St. Honoré. Joséphine and Jacques will be there.'

'I know,' she said quietly. 'They told me they were going. I have no influence to stop them.'

'You will be there, too?' he asked.

'Of course. So will poor Maman,' she replied simply.

'This may be the turning point, Régine,' he said with passionate earnestness, 'in the history of France!'

'I only remember that you, Bertrand, have probably spoken of your plan to Theresia Cabarrus, that the place will be swarming with the spies of Robespierre, and that you and the children will be recognized, seized, dragged into prison, then to the guillotine! My God!' she added, in a pitiful murmur. 'And I am powerless to do anything but look on whilst you run your rash heads into a noose, and then follow you all to death, whilst Maman is left alone to perish in misery and in want.'

'A pessimist again, Régine!' he said with a forced laugh, and in his turn rose to his feet. ' 'Tis little we have accomplished this evening,' he added bitterly, 'by talking.'

She said nothing more.

Silently she preceded him out of the little church porch, the habitual trysting-place, where at one time she had spent so many happy hours.

Less than five minutes after Bertrand and Régine had left the porch of Petit St. Antoine, the heavy oak door of the church was cautiously opened and presently the figure of a man emerged, hardly discernible in the gloom. He slipped through the door into the porch, then closed the former noiselessly behind him.

A moment or two later his huge, bulky figure was lumbering up the Rue St. Antoine, in the direction of the Arsenal, his down-at-heel shoes making a dull clip-clop on the cobblestones. The city gates were still open at this hour, for it was only a little while ago that the many church clocks of the quartier had struck eight, nor did the sergeant at the gate pay much heed to the beggarly caitiff who went by; only he and the half-dozen men of the National Guard who were in charge of the gate, did remark that the belated wayfarer appeared to be in distress with a terrible asthmatic cough which caused one of the men to say with grim facetiousness:

'Pardi! but here's a man who will not give maman guillotine any trouble!'

They all noticed, moreover, that after the asthmatic giant had passed through the city gate, he turned his shuffling footsteps in the direction of the Rue de la Planchette.

5 | Rascality rejoices

THE Fraternal Suppers were a great success. They were the invention of Robespierre, and the unusual warmth of these early spring evenings lent the support of their balmy atmosphere to the scheme.

All Paris is out in the streets on these mild April nights. Families out on a holiday, after the daily spectacle of the death-cart taking the enemies of the people, the conspirators against their liberty, to the guillotine.

The Rue St. Honoré is a typical example of what goes on all over the city. Though it is very narrow and therefore peculiarly inconvenient for the holding of outdoor entertainments, the Fraternal Suppers there are extensively patronized, because the street itself is consecrated as holding the house wherein lives Robespierre.

Here, as elsewhere, huge braziers are lit at intervals, so that materfamilias may cook the few herrings she has brought with her if she be so minded. All down the narrow street tables are set with resin torches, tallow candles, or old stable lanthorns here and there, adding picturesqueness to the scene which might otherwise have seemed sordid, with those pewter mugs and tin plates, the horn-handled knives and iron spoons.

The scanty light does little more than accentuate the darkness around, the deep shadows under projecting balconies or lintels of portes-cochères carefully closed and barred for the night; but it glints with weird will-o'-the-wisp-like fitfulness on crimson caps and tricolour cockades, on drawn and begrimed faces, bony arms, or lean, brown hands.

There is laughter around the festive boards, fun and frolic. Jokes are cracked, mostly of a grim order.

The provisions are scanty. Every family brings its own. Two or three herrings, sprinkled with shredded onions and wetted with a little vinegar, or else a few boiled prunes or a pottage of lentils and beans.

'Can you spare some of that bread, citizen?'

'Aye! if I can have a bite of your cheese.'

They are fraternal suppers! And the whole of it was Robespierre's idea. He conceived and carried it through, commanded the voices in the Convention that voted the money required for the tables, the benches, the tallow candles. He lives close by, in this very street, humbly, quietly, like a true son of the people, sharing house and board with citizen Duplay, the cabinet-maker, and with his family. A great man, Robespierre!

'You have heard him speak, citizen?'

A girl, still in her teens, her elbows resting on the table, her hands supporting her rounded chin, asks the question with bated breath. Her large grey eyes, hollow and glowing, are fixed upon a tall, ungainly creature, who sprawls over the table, vainly trying to dispose of his long limbs in a manner comfortable to himself.

His hair is lank and matted with grease, his face covered in coal-dust; a sennight's growth of beard, stubbly and dusty, accentuates the squareness of his jaw even whilst it fails to conceal altogether the cruel, sarcastic curves of his mouth. But for the moment, in the rapt eyes of the young enthusiast, he is a prophet, a seer, a human marvel: he has heard Robespierre speak.

'Was it in the club, citizen Rateau?' another woman asks.

'In the Club?' he says, and spits in a convenient direction to show his conempt for that or any other institution. 'I don't belong to any Club. There's no money in my pocket. And the Jacobins and the Cordeliers like to see a man with a decent coat on his back.'

T—B

His neighbours alongside the table, the young enthusiast opposite, the comely matron, paid no heed to him — waited in-
differently until the clumsy lout had regained his breath. Only
when he once more stretched out his long limbs, raised his head
and looked about him, panting and blear-eyed, did the girl
insist quietly:

'But you have heard *Him* speak!'

'Aye!' the ruffian replied dryly. 'I did.'

'When?'

'Night before last. Tenez! He was stepping out of citizen
Duplay's house yonder. He saw me leaning against the wall
close by. I was tired, half asleep, what? He spoke to me and
asked me where I lived.'

'Where you lived?' the girl echoed, disappointed.

'Was that all?' the matron added with a shrug of her shoulders.

The neighbours laughed.

The young enthusiast sighed, clasped her hands in fervour.

'He saw that you were poor, citizen Rateau,' she said with
conviction; 'and that you were tired. He wished to help and
comfort you. He never forgets. His eyes are upon you. He
knows your distress and that you are poor and weary. Leave it
to him, citizen Rateau. He will know how and when to help.'

'He will know, more like,' here broke in a harsh voice,
vibrating with excitement, 'how and when to lay his talons
on an obscure and helpless citizen whenever his batches for the
guillotine are insufficient to satisfy his lust!'

A dull murmur greeted this tirade. Only those who sat close
by the speaker knew which he was, for the lights were scanty
and burnt dim in the open air. The others only heard — received this arrow-shot aimed at their idol — with for the most
part a kind of dull resentment. The women were more loudly
indignant.

'Shame! Treason!'

'Guillotine, forsooth! The enemies of the people all deserve the guillotine!'

But from afar, down the street, there came one or two assenting cries.

'Well spoken, young man! As for me, I never trusted that bloodhound!'

'And a tyrant!' assented the original spokesman. 'His aim is a dictatorship, with his minions hanging around him like abject slaves. How are we better off now than in the days of kingship? Then, at least –'

But the speaker got no further. A hard crust of very dry black bread, aimed by a sure hand, caught him full in the face, whilst a hoarse voice shouted lustily:

'Hey there, citizen! If thou'lt not hold thy tongue 'tis thy neck that will be reeking with blood o'er soon, I'll warrant!'

'Well said, citizen Rateau!' put in another, speaking with his mouth full, but with splendid conviction. 'Every word uttered by that jackanapes yonder reeks of treason!'

'Where are the agents of the Committee of Public Safety? Men have been thrown into prison for less than this.'

'Denounce him!'

'Shame! Treason!' came soon from every side. Voices were raised all down the length of the tables. Some really felt indignation – burning, ferocious indignation; others only made a noise for the sheer pleasure of it, and because the past five years had turned cries of 'Treason!' and of 'Shame!' into a habit. Not that they knew what the disturbance was about.

So everyone cried 'Shame!' and 'Treason!' whilst those who had first dared to raise their voices against the popular demagogue drew together into a closer batch, trying no doubt to gather courage through one another's proximity. Eager, excited, a small compact group of two men – one a mere boy – and three women, it almost seemed as if they were suffering from some temporary hallucination.

In truth Bertrand Moncrif, face to face as he believed with martyrdom, was like one transfigured. Always endowed with good looks, he appeared like a veritable young prophet, haranguing the multitude and foretelling its doom.

Beside him Régine, motionless and white as a wraith, appeared alive only by her eyes, which were fixed on her beloved. In the hulking giant with the asthmatic cough she had recognized the man to whom she had ministered earlier in the day. Somehow, his presence here and now seemed to her sinister and threatening. It seemed as if all day he had been dogging her footsteps: first at the soothsayer's, then he surely must have followed her down the street. Then he had inspired her with pity; now his hideous face, his grimy hands, that croaking voice and churchyard cough, filled her with nameless terror.

With one arm she tried to press her brother Jacques closer to her breast, to quench his eagerness and silence his foolhardy tongue. But he, like a fierce, impatient young animal, fought to free himself from her loving embrace, shouted approval to Bertrand's oratory, heedless of Régine's warnings and of his mother's tears. Next to Régine, her sister Joséphine – a girl not out of her teens, with all the eagerness and exaggeration of extreme youth, was shouting quite as loudly as her brother Jacques, clapping her small hands together, turning glowing, defying, arrogant eyes on the crowd whom she hoped to sway with her ardour and her eloquence.

'Shame on us all!' she cried with passionate vehemence. 'Shame on us French women and French men, that we should be the abject slaves of such a bloodthirsty tyrant!'

Her mother, pale-faced, delicate, had obviously long since given up all hope of controlling this unruly little crowd. She was too listless, too anaemic, had no doubt suffered too much already, to be afraid for herself or for her children. She was past any thought of fear.

The Fraternal Supper threatened to end in a free fight,

wherein the only salvation for the young fire-eaters would lie in a swift taking to their heels. But Bertrand appeared unconscious of all danger.

'Shame on you all!' he called out loudly, and his fresh, sonorous voice rang out above the tumult and the hoarse murmurings. 'Shame on the people of France for bowing their necks to such monstrous tyranny. Citizens of Paris, think on it! Is not Liberty a mockery now? Do you call your bodies your own? They are but food for cannon at the bidding of the Convention. Your families? You are parted from those you love. Your wife. You are torn from her embrace. Your children? They are taken from you for the service of the State. And by whose orders? Tell me that! By whose orders, I say?'

This of course was the end – this folly, this mad, senseless, useless folly! Already through the gloom Régine could see as in a horrible vision all those she cared for dragged before a tribunal that knew of no mercy; she could hear the deathcarts rattling along the cobble-stones, she could see the hideous arms of the guillotine, ready to receive this unique, this beloved, this precious prey.

But for the fact that this was a 'Fraternal Supper', that people had come out here with their families, their young children, to eat and to make merry and to forget all their troubles as well as the pall of crime that hung over the entire city, I doubt not but what the young Hotspur and his crowd of rashlings would ere now have been torn from their seats, trampled under foot, at best been dragged to the nearest Commissary, as the asthmatic citizen Rateau had already threatened. As for Rateau, he just seemed to gather his huge limbs together, uttered an impatient oath and an angry: 'By all the cats and dogs that render this world hideous with their howls, I have had about enough of this screeching oratory.' Then he threw one long leg over the bench on which he had been sitting, and in an instant was lost in the gloom, only to reappear in the dim light a few seconds later, this time on the farther side of the table, immediately behind the young rhetorician, his ugly, begrimed face with its grinning, toothless mouth and his broad, bent shoulders towering above the other's slender figure.

'Knock him down, citizen!' a young woman cried excitedly. 'Hit him in the face! Silence his abominable tongue!'

But Bertrand was not to be silenced yet. No doubt the fever of notoriety, of martyrdom, had got into his blood.

'By whose orders,' he reiterated, with passionate vehemence, 'by whose orders are we, free citizens of France, dragged into this abominable slavery? Is it by those of the Representatives of the People? No! Your bodies, citizens, your freedom, your wives, your children, are the slaves, the property, the toys of one man – real tyrant and traitor; the oppressor of the weak, the enemy of the people; and that man is –'

Again he was interrupted, this time more forcibly. A terrific blow on the head deprived him of speech and of sight.

Whence the blow had come, Bertrand had no notion.

He had a swift vision of a giant form towering over him, with grimy fist uplifted and toothless mouth grinning hideously, and of the crowd, rising from their seats, turning their backs upon him, waving arms and caps frantically, and shouting, shouting with vociferous lustiness.

But the next moment these visions faded into complete oblivion. He felt something hard and heavy hitting him in the back. All the light, the faces, the outstretched hands, danced wildly before his eyes, and he sank like a log on the greasy pavement, dragging pewter plates, mugs and bottles down with him in his fall.

6 | *One crowded hour of glorious life*

AND all the while, the people were shouting:
'Robespierre!'
The Fraternal Supper was interrupted. Men and women
pushed and jostled and screamed, the while a small, spare figure
in dark cloth coat and immaculate breeches, with smooth brown
hair and pale, ascetic face, stood for a moment under the lintel
of a gaping porte-cochère. He had two friends with him; handsome, enthusiastic St. Just, the right hand and the spur of the
bloodthirsty monster, own kinsman to Armand St. Just the
renegade, whose sister was married to a rich English milord;
and Couthon, delicate, whose devotion to the tyrant was partly
made up of ambition, and wholly of genuine admiration.

At the uproarious cheering which greeted his appearance,
Robespierre advanced into the open, whilst a sudden swift light
of triumph darted from his narrow, pale eyes.

'And you still hesitate!' St. Just whispered excitedly in his
ear. 'Why, you hold the people absolutely in the hollow of
your hand!'

'Have patience, friend!' Couthon remonstrated quietly.
'Robespierre's hour is about to strike. To hasten it now, might
be courting disaster.'

Robespierre walked a few steps down the street, keeping close
to the houses on his left; his two friends, St. Just and Couthon
in his carrying chair, were immediately behind him.

Then, all of a sudden, the great man came to a halt, faced
the crowd, and with an impressive gesture imposed silence and
attention. His bodyguard cleared a space for him and he stood
in the midst of them, with the light of a resin torch striking

full upon his spare figure and bringing into bold relief that thin face so full of sinister expression, the cruel mouth and the coldly glittering eyes. He was looking straight across the table, on which the debris of Fraternal Suppers lay in unsavoury confusion.

On the other side of the table, Mme. de Serval with her three children sat, or rather crouched, closely huddled against one another. Joséphine was clinging to her mother, Jacques to Régine. The two young faces as well as that of Mme. de Serval appeared distorted and haggard, whilst Régine's eyes, dilated with terror, strove to meet Robespierre's steady gaze, which was charged with sinister mockery.

'And where is our eloquent orator of a while ago?' the great man asked quietly. 'I heard my name, for I sat at my window looking with joy on the fraternization of the people of France. I caught sight of the speaker, and came down to hear more clearly what he had to say. But where is he?'

His pale eyes wandered slowly along the crowd; and such was the power exercised by this extraordinary man, so great the terror that he inspired, that everyone there – men, women and children, workers and vagabonds – turned their eyes away, dared not meet his glance lest in it they read an accusation or a threat.

Indeed, no one dared to speak. The young rhetorician had disappeared, and everyone trembled lest they should be implicated in his escape. He had evidently got away under cover of the confusion and the noise. But his companions were still there – four of them; the woman and the boy and the two girls, crouching like frightened beasts before the obvious fury, the certain vengeance of the people.

Robespierre's cruel, appraising glance rested on those four pathetic forms, so helpless, so desperate, so terrified.

'Citizens,' he said coldly, 'did you not hear me ask where your eloquent companion is at this moment?'

Régime alone knew that he lay like a dog under the table,

close to her feet, but at the ominous query she pressed her trembling lips close together, whilst Joséphine and Jacques clung to her with the strength of despair.

'Do not parley with the rabble, citizen,' St. Just whispered eagerly. 'This is a grand moment for you. Let the people of their own accord condemn those who dared to defame you.'

The people, in truth, were over-ready to take vengeance into their own hands.

'À la lanterne, les aristos!'

Gaunt, bedraggled forms leaned across the table, shook be-grimed fists in the direction of the four crouching figures. They retreated into the shadows step by step, as those threatening fists appeared to draw closer, clutching at the nearest table and dragging it with them, in an altogether futile attempt at a barricade.

Robespierre, like an avenging wraith, theatrical yet impassive, stood in the light of a huge resin torch, which threw alternate lights and shadows, grotesque and weird, upon his meagre figure.

'À la lanterne!' the people – more especially the women – demanded insistently.

Robespierre turned to one of his bodyguard.

'Take the aristos to the nearest Commissariat,' he said. 'I'll have no bloodshed to mar our Fraternal Supper.'

How it all happened after that, none who were there could in truth have told you. The darkness, the flickering light, the glow of the braziers, which made the inky blackness around more pronounced, made everything indistinguishable to ordinary human sight. Certain it is that citizen Rateau – who had constituted himself the spokesman of the mob – was at one time seen towering behind the four unfortunates, with his huge arms stretched out, his head thrown back, his mouth wide open, screaming abuse and vituperation, demanding the people's right to take the law into its own sovereign hands.

At that moment the light of the nearest resin torch threw his hulking person into bold relief against a heavy porte-cochère which was immediately behind him. The next instant a puff of wind blew the flame of the torch in a contrary direction, and darkness suddenly enevloped the ranting colossus and the cowering prey already to his hand.

'Rateau!' shouted someone.

'Hey, there! citizen Rateau! Where art thou?' came soon from every side.

No answer came from the spot where Rateau had last been seen, and it seemed as if just then a strong current of air had slammed a heavy door to somewhere in the gloom. Citizen Rateau had disappeared, and the four traitors along with him.

It took a few seconds of valuable time ere the mob suspected that it was being robbed of its prey. Then a huge upheaval occurred, a motion of the human mass densely packed in the Rue St. Honoré, that was not unlike the rush of water through a narrow gorge.

'Rateau!' People were yelling the name from end to end of the street.

Then the whole crowd oscillated in the direction of the mysterious porte-cochère. Those who were in the front ranks threw themselves against the heavy panels, whilst those in the rear pushed with all their might. But the portes-cochères of old Paris are heavily constructed. Woodwork that had resisted the passage of centuries withheld the onslaught of a pack of half-starved caitiffs. But only for a while.

The mob, fearing that it was getting foiled, broke into a howl of execration, and Robespierre, his face more drawn and grey than before, turned to his companions, trying to read their thoughts.

Already the massive oak panels were yielding to persistent efforts. The mighty woodwork began to crack under the pressure of this living battering ram; when suddenly the howls of those who were in the rear turned to a wild cry of delight. Those who were pushing against the porte-cochère paused in their task. All necks were suddenly craned upwards.

There, some few metres lower down the street, on the third-floor balcony of a neighbouring house, the figure of Rateau had just appeared. The window immediately behind him was wide open and the room beyond was flooded with light, so that his huge person appeared distinctly silhouetted – a black and gargantuan mass – against the vivid and glowing background. His lank hair fluttered in the breeze, his huge chest was bare and his ragged shirt hung in tatters from his brawny arms.

Flung across his left shoulder, he held an inanimate female form, whilst with his right hand he dragged another through the open window in his wake. Just below him, a huge brazier was shedding its crimson glow.

For the space of two seconds only did he stand there, in full view of the crowd, in full view of the almighty tyrant whose defamation he had sworn to avenge. Then he cried in stentorian tones:

'Thus perish all conspirators against the liberty of the people, all traitors to its cause, by the hands of the people and for the glory of their chosen!'

And, with a mighty twist of his huge body, he picked up the inanimate forms that lay lifeless at his feet. For a moment he held the two in his arms, high above the iron railing of the balcony; for a moment those two lifeless, shapeless forms hung in the darkness in mid-air, whilst an entire crowd of fanatics held their breath and waited, awed and palpitating, only to break out into frantic cheering as the giant hurled the two lifeless bodies down, straight into the glowing brazier.

'Two more to follow!' he shouted lustily.

There was pushing and jostling and cheering. Women screamed, men blasphemed and children cried. Shouts of 'Vive

Rateau!' mingled with those of 'Vive Robespierre!' A circle was formed, hands holding hands, and a wild saraband danced around the glowing brazier. And this mad orgy of enthusiasm lasted for full three minutes, until the foremost among those who, awestruck and horrified, had approached the brazier in order to see the final agony of the abominable traitor, burst out with a prolonged 'Malediction!'

Beyond that exclamation, they were speechless – pointed with trembling hands at the shapeless bundles on which the dull fire of the braziers had not yet obtained a purchase.

The bundles were shapeless indeed. Rags hastily tied together to represent human forms; but rags only! The people had been fooled, hideously fooled by a traitor all the more execrable, as he had seemed one of themselves.

'Malediction! Death to the traitor!'

They looked up to that third-floor balcony which had so fascinated them a while ago. But now the window was shut and no light from within chased the gloom that hung over the houses around.

'Rateau!' the people shouted.

But Rateau had disappeared.

The house from whence he had thus mocked and flouted the people was searched through and through by a mob who found nothing but bare boards and naked walls, empty rooms and disused cupboards on which to wreak its fury.

But down there, lying on the top of the brazier, were those two bundles of rags slowly being consumed by the smouldering embers, silent proofs of the existence of that hulking creature whose size and power had, with that swiftness peculiar to human conceptions, already become legendary.

And in a third-floor room, a lamp that had recently been extinguished, a coil of rope, more rags, male and female clothes, a pair of boots, a battered hat, were mute witnesses to the swift passage of the mysterious giant with the wheezy cough – the trickster who had fooled a crowd and thrown the great Robespierre himself into ridicule.

7 | *Two interludes*

Two hours later the Rue St. Honoré had resumed its habitual graveyard-like stillness. The stillness had to come at last.

Here, as in other quarters of Paris, the fraternal suppers had come to an end; and perspiring matrons, dragging weary children at their skirts, wended their way homewards; whilst their men went to consummate the evening's entertainment at one of the numerous clubs or cabarets where the marvellous doings in the Rue St. Honoré could be comfortably lived over again or retailed to those, less fortunate, who had not been there to see.

And so the streets were entirely deserted, save here and there for the swift passage of a furtive form, hugging the walls, with hands in pockets and crimson cap pulled over the eyes, anxious only to escape the vigilance of the night-watchman, swift of foot and silent of tread; and anon, in the Rue St. Honoré itself, when even these nightbirds had ceased to flutter, the noiseless movement of a dark and mysterious form that stirred cautiously upon the greasy cobble-stones. More silent, more furtive than any hunted beast creeping out of its lair, this mysterious form emerged from under one of the tables that was standing nearly opposite the house where Robespierre lived and close to the one where the superhuman colossus had wrought his magic trick.

It was Bertrand Moncrif. His senses still reeling, his limbs cramped and aching, he had lain stark and still under the table just where he had fallen, not sufficiently conscious to realize what was happening beyond his very limited range of vision or to marvel what was the ultimate fate of his companions.

It was only when the silence around had lasted an eternity of time that he ventured out of his hiding-place. With utmost caution, hardly daring to breathe, he crept on hands and knees and looked about him, up and down the street. There was no one about.

Bertrand struggled to his feet, smothering a cry of pain. His head ached furiously, his knees shook under him; but he managed to crawl as far as the nearest house, and rested for a while against its wall.

He ventured to look fearfully up and down the street. Tables scattered pell-mell, the unsavoury remnants of fraternal suppers, a couple of smouldering braziers, collectively met his gaze. And, at one point, sprawling across a table, with head lost between outstretched arms, a figure, apparently asleep, perhaps dead.

The figure did not move, and gradually Bertrand nerved himself up to confidence and then to action. He buried his head in the folds of his coat-collar and his hands in the pockets of his breeches, and with silent, stealthy footsteps he started to make his way down the street. At first he looked back once or twice at the immobile figure sprawling across the table. It had not moved, still appeared as if it might be dead. Then Bertrand took to his heels and, no longer looking either behind him or to the right or left, with elbows pressed close to his side, he started to run in the direction of the Tuileries.

A minute later, the motionless figure came back to life, rose quickly and with swift, noiseless tread, started to run in the same direction . . .

In the cabarets throughout the city, the chief topic of conversation was the mysterious event of the Rue St. Honoré. Those who had seen it all had marvellous tales to tell of the hero of the adventure.

'The man was eight or else nine feet high; his arms reached right across the street from house to house. Flames spurted out of his mouth when he coughed. He had horns on his head; cloven feet; a forked tail!'

But all agreed that the mysterious giant was in truth none other than the far-famed Englishman – that spook, that abominable trickster, that devil incarnate, known to the Committees as the Scarlet Pimpernel.

'But how could it be the Englishman?' was suddenly put forward by citizen Hotot, the picturesque landlord of the Cabaret de la Liberté, a well-known rendezvous close to the Carrousel. 'How could it be the Englishman who played you that trick, seeing that you all say it was citizen Rateau who . . . The devil take it all!' he added, and scratched his bald head with savage vigour.

'It was the Englishman, I tell thee!' one of his customers asserted indignantly. 'Ask anyone who saw him!'

'And *I* tell thee,' broke in citizen Sical, the butcher. 'I tell thee that it was citizen Rateau. Don't I know citizen Rateau?' he added, and brought that heavy fist of his down upon the upturned cask on which stood pewter mugs and bottles of eau de vie, and glared aggressively round upon the assembly.

One man alone was bold enough to take up the challenge – a wizened little fellow, a printer by trade, with skin of the texture of grained oak and a few unruly curls that tumbled over one another above a highly polished forehead.

'And I tell thee, citizen Sical,' he said with firm decision; 'I tell thee and those who aver, as thou dost, that citizen Rateau had anything to do with those monkey-tricks, that ye lie. Because –' He paused and glanced around him, like a clever actor conscious of the effect which he produced. His tiny beady eyes blinked in the glare of the lamp before him.

'Because what?' came in an eager chorus from every side.

'Because,' resumed the other sententiously, 'all the while that ye were supping at the expense of the State in the open, and had your gizzards stirred by the juggling of some unknown mountebank, citizen Rateau was lying comfortably drunk and snoring lustily in the antechamber of Mother Théot, the sooth-sayer, right at the other end of Paris!'

'How do you know that, citizen Langlois?' queried the host with icy reproval, for butcher Sical was his best customer, and Sical did not like being contradicted. But little Langlois with the shiny forehead and tiny, beady, humorous eyes, continued unperturbed.

'Pardi!' he said gaily, 'because I was at Mother Théot's my-self, and saw him there.'

And Langlois told all he knew. How he had gone to Mother Théot's at about four o'clock in the afternoon, and had sat patiently waiting beside his friend Rateau, who wheezed and snored alternately for a couple of hours. How, at six o'clock or a little after, Rateau went out because – the aristo, forsooth! – had found the atmosphere filthy in Mother Théot's ante-chamber – no doubt he went to get another drink.

'At about half-past seven,' the little printer went on glibly, 'my turn came to speak with the old witch. When I came out it was long past eight o'clock and quite dark. I saw Rateau sprawling upon a bench, half asleep. I tried to speak with him, but he only grunted. However, I went out then to get a bit of supper at one of the open-air places, and at ten o'clock I was once more past Mother Théot's place. One or two people were coming out of the house. They were all grumbling because they had been told to go. Rateau was one who was for making a disturbance, but I took him by the arm. We went down the street together, and parted company in the Rue de l'Anier, where he lodges. And here I am!' concluded Langlois, and turned triumphantly to challenge the gaze of every one of the sceptics around him.

There was not a single doubtful point in his narrative, and though he was questioned – aye! and severely cross-questioned, too – he never once swerved from his narrative or in any manner did he contradict himself. Later on it transpired that there were others who had been in Mother Théot's antechamber that day. They too subsequently corroborated all that the little printer had said. One of them was the wife of Sical's own brother; and there were others. So, what would you?

'Name of a name of a dog, then, who was it who spirited the aristos away?'

8 | *The beautiful Spaniard*

IN the Rue Villedot, which is in the Louvre quarter of Paris, there is a house, stone built and five-storied, with grey shutters to all the windows and balconies of wrought iron – a house exactly similar to hundreds and thousands of others in every quarter of Paris. During the day the small wicket in the huge porte-cochère is usually kept open; it allows a peep into a short dark passage, and beyond it to the lodge of the concierge. Beyond this again there is a courtyard, into which, from every one of its four sides, five rows of windows, all adorned with grey shutters, blink down like so many colourless eyes.

On the left of the entrance passage and opposite the lodge of the concierge there is a tall glass door, and beyond it the vestibule and primary staircase, which gives access to the principal apartments – those that look out upon the street and are altogether more luxurious and more airy than those which give upon the courtyard. To the latter, two back stairways give access. They are at the far corners of the courtyard; both are pitch dark and reek of stuffiness and evil smells. The apartments which they serve, especially those on the lower floors, are dependent for light and air on what modicum of these gifts of heaven comes down the shaft into the quadrangle.

After dark, of course, porte-cochère and wicket are both closed, and if a belated lodger or visitor desires to enter the house, he must ring the bell and the concierge in his lodge will pull a communicating cord that will unlatch the wicket. It is up to the belated visitor or lodger to close the wicket after him, and he is bound by law to give his name, together with the number of the apartment to which he is going, in to the concierge as he goes past the lodge. The concierge, on the other hand, will take a look at him so that he may identify him should trouble or police inquiry arise.

On this night of April, somewhere near midnight, there was a ring at the outer door. Citizen Leblanc, the concierge, roused from his first sleep, pulled the communicating cord. A young man, hatless and in torn coat and muddy boots and breeches, slipped in through the wicket and hurried past the lodge, giving only one name, but that in a clear voice, as he passed:

'Citoyenne Cabarrus.'

The concierge turned over in his bed and grunted, half asleep. His duty clearly was to run after the visitor, who had failed to give his own name; but to begin with, the worthy concierge was very tired; and then the name which the belated caller had given was one requiring special consideration. The citoyenne Cabarrus was young and well-favoured, and even in these troublous days, youth and beauty demanded certain privileges which no patriotic concierge could refuse to grant. Obviously, therefore, it was best not to pry too closely into secrets, the keeping of which might prove uncomfortable for one's peace of mind.

And so the belated visitor was able to make his way across the courtyard and up the dark back stairs unmolested.

Up the dark and narrow staircase he hurried, dizzy and sick, his head reeling in the dank atmosphere, his shaking hands seeking the support of the walls as he climbed wearily up to the third floor. Here he almost measured his length upon the landing, tottered up again and came down sprawling on his knees against one of the doors – the one which had the number 22 painted upon it. He had not sufficient strength to stretch out an arm in order to ring the bell, but only beat feebly against the panel of the door with his moist palm.

A moment later the door was opened, and the unfortunate fell forward into the vestibule at the feet of a tall apparition clad in white and holding a small table lamp above her head. The apparition gave a little scream, hastily put down the lamp, and by retreating forcefully farther into the vestibule dragged the half-animate form of the young man along too; for he was now clinging to a handful of white skirt with the strength of despair.

'I am lost, Theresia!' he moaned pitiably. 'Hide me, for God's sake! . . .'

Theresia Cabarrus made no attempt to raise the crouching figure from the ground. Anon she called loudly: 'Pepita!' and whilst waiting for an answer to this call, she remained quite still, and the frown of puzzlement on her face yielded to one of fear.

The next moment an old woman came from somewhere out of the darkness, threw up her hands at sight of that grovelling figure on the floor, and would no doubt have broken out in loud lament but that her young mistress ordered her at once to close the door.

'Then help the citoyen Moncrif to a sofa in my room,' the

beautiful Theresia went on. 'Give him a restorative and see above all to it that he holds his tongue!'

With a quick jerk she freed herself from the convulsive grasp of the young man, and walked quickly across the small vestibule, leaving the unfortunate Moncrif to the ministrations of Pepita. Theresia Cabarrus was, in this year 1794, in her twenty-fourth year, and perhaps in the zenith of her beauty. At this moment, in the sparsely furnished room of her dingy apartment, she looked like an angry goddess.

After a while Pepita came back.

'Well?' queried Theresia impatiently.

'Poor M. Bertrand is very ill,' the old Spanish woman replied with unconcealed sympathy. 'He has fever. Bed is the only place for him . . .'

'He cannot stay here, as thou well knowest, Pepita,' the imperious beauty retorted. 'Thy head and mine are in danger every moment that he spends under this roof.'

'But thou couldst not turn a sick man out into the streets in the middle of the night.'

'Why not?' Theresia replied coldly.

'Because he would die on thy doorstep.'

Theresia shrugged her shoulders.

'He dies if he goes,' she said slowly, 'and we die if he stays. Tell him to go, Pepita, ere citizen Tallien comes.'

A shudder went through the old woman's spare frame.

'It is late,' she protested. 'Citizen Tallien will not come to-night.'

'Not only he,' Theresia rejoined coldly, 'but – but – the other – Thou knowest well, Pepita – those two arranged to meet here in my lodgings tonight.'

'But not at this hour!'

'After the sitting of the Convention.'

'It is nearly midnight. They'll not come,' the old woman persisted obstinately.

'They arranged to meet here, to talk over certain matters which interest their party,' citoyenne Cabarrus went on, equally firmly. 'They'll not fail. So tell citizen Moncrif to go, Pepita. He endangers my life by staying here.'

'Then do the dirty work thyself,' the old woman muttered sullenly. 'I'll not be a party to cold-blooded murder.'

'Well, since citizen Moncrif's life is more valuable to thee than mine –' Theresia began, but got no further.

Bertrand Moncrif, very pale, still looking scared and wild, had quietly entered the room.

'You wish me to go, Theresia,' he said simply. 'You did not think surely that I would do anything that might endanger your safety. My God!' he added with passionate vehemence, 'Do you not know that I would at any time lay down my life for yours?'

Theresia shrugged her beautiful shoulders.

'Of course, of course, Bertrand,' she said a little impatiently, though obviously trying to be kind. 'But I do entreat you not to go into heroics at this hour, and not to put on tragic airs. You must see that for yourself as well as for me it would be fatal if you were found here, and –'

'And I am going, Theresia,' he broke in seriously. 'I ought never to have come. I was a fool, as usual!' he added with bitterness. 'But after that awful fracas I was dazed and hardly knew what I was doing.'

The frown of vexation reappeared upon the woman's fair, smooth brow.

'The fracas?' she asked quickly. 'What fracas?'

'In the Rue St. Honoré. I thought you knew.'

'No. I know nothing,' she retorted, and her voice now was trenchant and hard. 'What happened?'

'They were deifying that brute Robespierre –'

'Silence!' she broke in harshly. 'Name no names.'

'They were deifying a bloodthirsty tyrant, and I –'

'And you rose from your seat,' she broke in again, and this

time with a laugh that was cruel in its biting irony; 'and lashed yourself into a fury of eloquent vituperation. Oh, I know! I know!' she went on excitedly. 'You and your Fatalists, or whatever you call yourselves! And that rage of martyrdom!'

Bertrand tried to pacify her.

'I am going,' he said earnestly. 'Theresia, my beloved, try to forgive me.'

'No, no!' she murmured in a hoarse whisper. 'Don't go just yet . . . not before Pepita has seen if the stairs are clear.'

The old woman's footsteps were heard hurrying back. Theresia smothered a desperate cry of warning as Bertrand strode rapidly through the door and across the vestibule only to be met here by Pepita, who pushed him with all her might incontinently back.

'Citizen Tallien,' Pepita had murmured hurriedly. 'He is on the landing. Come this way.'

She dragged Bertrand by the arm, not waiting for orders from her mistress this time, along a narrow dark passage, which at its extreme end gave access to a tiny kitchen. Into this she pushed him and locked the door upon him.

Citoyenne Cabarrus had not moved. Her eyes, dilated with terror, mutely questioned the old woman as the latter made ready to admit the visitor. Pepita gave reply as best she could, by silent gestures, indicating the passage and the action of turning a key in the lock.

Theresia pulled herself together. Obviously the old woman's warning was not to be ignored, nor had it been given a moment too soon. Outside, the visitor had renewed his impatient rat-tat against the door. The eyes of mistress and maid met for one brief second. Theresia was rapidly regaining her presence of mind; whereupon Pepita smoothed out her apron, readjusted her cap, and went to open the door, even whilst Theresia said in a firm voice, loudly enough for the new visitor to hear:

'One of my guests, at last! Open quickly, Pepita!'

9 | *A hideous, fearful hour*

A YOUNG man – tall, spare, with sallow skin and shifty, rest-less eyes – pushed unceremoniously past the old servant, threw his hat and cane down on the nearest chair, and hurrying across the vestibule, entered the salon where the beautiful Spaniard, a picture of serene indifference, sat ready to receive him.

'Ah, citizen Tallien!' the fair Theresia exclaimed. 'You are the first to arrive, and are indeed welcome. Well!' she added, with a provocative smile, and extended a gracious arm in his direction. 'Are you not going to kiss my hand?'

'I heard a voice,' was all the response he gave. 'A man's voice. Whose was it?'

Her eyes became as round and as innocent-looking as a child's.

'A man's voice?' she asked with a perfect air of astonish-ment. 'You are crazy, mon ami; or else are crediting my faithful Pepita with a virile bass, which in truth she doth not possess!'

'Whose voice was it?' Tallien reiterated, making an effort to speak calmly.

Whereupon the fair Theresia, no longer gracious or arch, looked him up and down as if he were no better than a lackey.

'Ah, ça!' she rejoined coldly. 'Are you perchance trying to cross-question me? By what right, I pray you, citizen Tallien, do you assume this hectoring tone in my presence? I am not yet your wife, remember; and 'tis not you, I imagine, who are the dictator of France.'

'Do not tease me, Theresia!' the man interposed hoarsely. 'Bertrand Moncrif is here.'

For the space of a second, or perhaps less, Theresia gave

no reply to the taunt. Her quick, alert brain had already faced possibilities, and she was far too clever a woman to take the risks which a complete evasion of the truth would have entailed at this moment.

'I am not teasing you, citizen. Bertrand came here for shelter a while ago.'

Tallien drew a sigh of satisfaction, and she went on:

'But, obviously, I could not keep him here. He seemed hurt and frightened . . . He has been gone this past half-hour.'

For a moment it seemed as if the man, in face of this obvious lie, would flare out into a hot retort; but Theresia's luminous eyes subdued him, and before the cool contempt expressed by those exquisite lips, he felt all his blustering courage oozing away.

'The man is an abominable and an avowed traitor,' he said sullenly. 'Only two hours ago –'

'I know,' she broke in coldly. 'He vilified Robespierre. A dangerous thing to do. Bertrand was ever a fool, and he lost his head.'

'He will lose it more effectually tomorrow,' Tallien retorted grimly.

'You mean that you would denounce him?'

'That I *will* denounce him. I would have done so tonight, before coming here, only – only –'

'Only what?'

'I was afraid he might be here.'

Theresia broke into a ringing if somewhat artificial peal of laughter.

'I must thank you, citizen, for this consideration of my feelings. It was, in truth, thoughtful of you to think of sparing me a scandal. But, since Bertrand is *not* here –'

'I know where he lodges. He'll not escape, citoyenne. My word on it!'

In answer to his last threatening words, the lovely Theresia rejoined more seriously:

'So as to make sure I do not escape either! Moncrif, you say, is an avowed traitor. Has openly vilified and insulted your demi-god. He has been seen coming to my apartments. Good! I tell you that he is no longer here. But let that pass. He is denounced. Good! Sent to the guillotine. Good again! And Theresia Cabarrus in whose house he tried to seek refuge, much against her will, goes to the guillotine in his company. The prospect may please you, mon ami, because for the moment you are suffering from a senseless attack of jealousy. But I confess that it does not appeal to me.'

The man was silent now; awed against his will. Insane jealously was fighting a grim fight in his heart with terror for his beloved. Her argument was a sound one. Powerful though he was in the Convention, his influence was as nothing compared with that of Robespierre. And he knew his redoubtable colleague well enough to know that an insult such as Moncrif had put upon him in the Rue St. Honoré this night would never be forgiven.

Theresia Cabarrus was clever enough and quick enough to see that she had gained one point.

'Come and kiss my hand,' she said, with a little sigh of satisfaction.

This time the man obeyed, without an instant's hesitation.

She settled herself down more comfortably upon the settee, and graciously allowed him to sit on a low chair beside her.

The turbulent little incident was closed.

'You will help me, Theresia?' he pleaded.

She nodded, and asked coldly: 'How?'

'You know that Robespierre suspects me,' he went on, and instinctively, at the mere breathing of that awe-inspiring name his voice sank to a murmur. 'Ever since I came back from Bordeaux.'

'I know. Your leniency there is attributed to me.'

'Robespierre never forgives,' he rejoined vaguely. 'And he had sent me to Bordeaux to punish, not to pardon.'

'Then you *are* afraid!' she insisted. 'Has anything happened?'

'No; only his usual hints – his vague threats. You know them.'

She nodded.

'I would not fear, Theresia,' he protested, and there was a note of tender reproach in his voice, 'if it were not for you.'

'I know that, mon ami,' she rejoined. 'Well, what do you want me to do?'

He leaned forward in his chair.

'There are two things,' he said insinuatingly, 'which you could do, Theresia, either of which would place Robespierre under such lasting obligation to you that he would admit us into the inner circle of his friends, trust us and confide in us as he does in St. Just or Couthon.'

'Well?' she rejoined. 'What are these two things?'

He paused a moment, appeared to hesitate; then said resolutely:

'Robespierre will be here directly. Bertrand Moncrif is here – why not deliver the young traitor, and earn Robespierre's gratitude?'

'Oh!' she broke in in indignant protest. Then, as she caught the look of jealous anger which suddenly flared up in his narrow eyes again, she went on with a careless shrug of her shoulders: 'Bertrand is not here, as I told you, my friend. So these means of serving your cause are out of my reach.'

'Theresia,' he urged, 'by deceiving me –'

'By tantalizing me,' she broke in harshly, 'you do yourself no good. Let us understand one another, my friend,' she went on more gently. 'You wish me to serve you by serving the dictator of France. And I tell you you'll not gain your ends by taunting me.'

'Theresia, we must make friends with Robespierre! He has the power; he rules over France. Whilst I –'

'Ah!' she retorted with vehemence. 'That is where you and your weak-kneed friends are wrong! You say that Robespierre rules France. 'Tis not true. It is not Robespierre, the man, who rules, it is his name! It rules by the fear which it evokes and by the slavery which it compels under the perpetual threat of death. Believe me,' she insisted, ' 'tis not Robespierre who rules, but the guillotine which he wields! And we are all of us helpless – you and I and your friends. And all the others who long to see the end of this era of bloodshed and of revenge, we have got to do as he tells us – pile up crime upon crime, massacre upon massacre, and bear the odium of it all, while he stands aloof in darkness and in solitude, the brain that guides, whilst you and your party are only the hands that strike. Oh! the humiliation of it! And if you were but men, all of you, instead of puppets –'

'Hush, Theresia, in heaven's name!' Tallien broke in at last. His ears, attuned to sensitiveness by an ever-present danger, had caught a sound which proceeded from the vestibule – a sound which made him shudder – a footstep – the opening of a door – a voice. 'Hush!' he entreated. 'Every dumb wall has ears, these days!'

'You are right, my friend,' she said under her breath. 'What do I care, after all? What do any of us care now, so long as our necks are fairly safe upon our shoulders? But I'll not sell Bertrand,' she added firmly. 'If I did it I should despise myself too much and hate you worse. So tell me quickly what else I can do to propitiate the ogre!'

'He'll tell you himself,' Tallien murmured hurriedly, as the sounds in the vestibule became more loud and distinctive. 'Here they are! And, in heaven's name, Theresia, remember that our lives are at that one man's mercy!'

10 | *The grim idol that the world adores*

PEPITA admitted into her mistress's apartments a singular group, composed of two able-bodied men supporting a palsied one. One of the former was St. Just, one of the most romantic figures of the Revolutionary period, the confidant and intimate friend of Robespierre and own cousin to Armand St. Just and to the beautiful Marguerite, who had married the fastidious English milord, Sir Percy Blakeney. The other was Chauvelin, at one time one of the most influential members of the Committee of Public Safety, now little more than a hanger-on of Robespierre's party. The palsied man was Couthon, despite his crimes an almost pathetic figure in his helplessness, after his friends had deposited him in an arm-chair and wrapped a rug around his knees.

Close behind these three men came Robespierre.

He dominated the small assembly, even though he sat for the most part silent. Immaculately dressed in blue cloth coat and white breeches, with clean linen at throat and wrist, his hair neatly tied back with a black silk bow, his nails polished, his shoes free from mud, he presented a marked contrast to the ill-conditioned appearance of these other products of revolutionary ideals.

St. Just, on the other hand – young, handsome, a brilliant talker and convinced enthusiast – was only too willing to air his compelling eloquence, was in effect the mouthpiece of the great man as he was his confidant and his right hand.

Then there was Couthon, sarcastic and contemptuous, delightful to tease Tallien and to effect a truculent manner, which brought abject flattery from the other's lips.

St. Just, the fiery young demagogue, and Couthon, the half-paralysed enthusiast, were known to be pushing their leader towards the proclamation of a triumvirate, with Robespierre as chief dictator and themselves as his two hands; and it amused the helpless cripple to see just how far the obsequiousness of Tallien and his colleagues would go in subscribing to so monstrous a project.

As for Chauvelin, he said very little, and the deference wherewith he listened to the others bore testimony to the humiliating subservience to which he had sunk.

And the beautiful Theresia, presiding over the small assembly like a goddess who listens to the prattle of men, sat for the most part quite still, on the one dainty piece of furniture of which her dingy apartment boasted.

St. Just was the first to give a serious turn to the conversation. The fraternal suppers had been alluded to with servile eulogy of the giant brain who had conceived the project.

Then it was that St. Just broke into a euphemistic account of the disorderly scene in the Rue St. Honoré

Theresia Cabarrus, roused from her queen-like indifference, at once became interested.

'The young traitor!' she exclaimed, with a great show of indignation. 'Who was he? What was he like?'

Couthon gave quite a minute description of Bertrand, an accurate one, too. He had faced the blasphemer for fully five minutes, and despite the flickering and deceptive light, had studied his features, distorted by fury and hate, and was quite sure that he would know them again.

Theresia listened eagerly, caught every inflection of the voices as they discussed the strange events that followed. The keenest observer there could not have detected the slightest agitation in her large, velvety eyes – not even when they met Robespierre's coldly inquiring gaze.

At one time she turned boldly to Tallien.

'You were there, too, citizen,' she said provokingly. 'Did *you* not recognize any of the traitors?'

Tallien stammered out an evasive answer, implored her with a look not to taunt him and not play like a thoughtless child within sight and hearing of a man-eating tiger. Theresia's dalliance with the young and handsome Bertrand must in truth be known to Robespierre's army of spies, and he – Tallien – was not altogether convinced that the fair Spaniard, despite her assurances to the contrary, was not harbouring Moncrif in her apartment even now.

Therefore he would not meet her tantalizing glance; and she, delighted to tease, threw herself with greater zest than before into the discussion, amused to see sober Tallien, whom in her innermost heart she despised, enduring tortures of apprehension.

'Ah!' she exclaimed, apparently enraptured by St. Just's glowing account of the occurrence, 'what would I not give to have seen it all!'

'Especially,' added Couthon, 'the spiriting away of the company of traitors through the agency of that mysterious giant, who some aver was just a coal-heaver named Rateau, whilst others vow that he was –'

'Name him not, friend Couthon,' St. Just broke in with a sarcastic chuckle. 'I pray thee, spare the feelings of citizen Chauvelin.'

Chauvelin made no retort, pressed his thin lips more tightly together as if to smother any incipient expression of the resentment which he felt.

'Ah, yes!' here interposed Tallien unctuously. 'Citizen Chauvelin has had one or two opportunities of measuring his prowess against that of the mysterious Englishman; but we are told that, despire his great talents, he has met with no success in that direction.'

'Do not tease our modest friend Chauvelin, I pray you

citizen,' Theresia broke in gaily. 'The Scarlet Pimpernel – that is the name of the mysterious Englishman, is it not? – is far more elusive and a thousand times more resourceful and daring than any mere man can possibly conceive. 'Tis a woman's wits that will bring him to his knees one day. You may take my word for that!'

'*Your* wits, citoyenne?'

Robespierre had spoken. It was the first time, since the discussion had turned on the present subject, that he had opened his lips.

She returned his glance, with provoking coolness, shrugged her splendid shoulders, and retorted airily:

'Oh, you want a woman with some talent as a sleuth-hound – a female counterpart of citizen Chauvelin. I have no genius in that direction.'

'Why not?' Robespierre went on dryly. 'You, fair citoyenne, would be well qualified to deal with the Scarlet Pimpernel, seeing that your adorer, Bertrand Moncrif, appears to be a protégé of the mysterious League.'

At this taunt, uttered by the dictator with deliberate emphasis, like one who knows what he is talking about, Tallien gave a gasp and his sallow cheeks became the colour of lead. But Theresia placed her cool, reassuring hand upon his.

'Bertrand Moncrif,' she said serenely, 'is no adorer of mine. He forswore his allegiance to me on the day that I plighted my troth to citizen Tallien.'

'That is as may be,' Robespierre retorted coldly. 'But he certainly was the leader of the gang of traitors whom that meddlesome English rabble chose to snatch away tonight from the vengeance of a justly incensed populace.'

'How do you know that, citizen Robespierre?' Theresia asked. 'Why do you suppose, citizen,' she insisted, 'that Bertrand Moncrif had anything to do with the fracas tonight?

Methought he had emigrated to England – or somewhere,'
she added airily.

'Did you think that, citoyenne?' Robespierre rejoined with
a wry smile. 'Then let me tell you that you are under a mis-
apprehension. Moncrif, the traitor, was the leader of the gang
that tried to rouse the people against me tonight. You ask me
how I know it?' he added icily. 'Well, I saw him – that is all!'

'Ah!' exclaimed Theresia, in well-played mild astonishment.
'You saw Bertrand Moncrif, citizen? He is in Paris, then?'

'Seemingly.'

'Strange, he never came to see me!'

'Strange, indeed!'

'What does he look like? Some people have told me that he
is getting fat.'

The discussion had now resolved itself into a duel between
these two: the ruthless dictator, sure of his power, and the
beautiful woman, conscious of hers. The atmosphere of the
drabbily furnished room had become electrical.

The one that really suffered throughout, and suffered acutely,
was Tallien. He would have given all that he possessed to know
for a certainty that Bertrand Moncrif was no longer in the
house.

'I entreat you, citizen Robespierre,' Theresia said, with a pout,
'to tell me if Bertrand Moncrif has grown fat.'

'That I cannot tell you, citoyenne,' Robespierre replied
curtly. 'Having recognized my enemy, I no longer paid heed
to him. My attention was arrested by his rescuer –'

'That elusive Scarlet Pimpernel,' she broke in gaily. 'Ah,
would I had been there!'

'I would you had, citoyenne,' he retorted. 'You would have
realized that to refuse your help to unmask an abominable spy
after such an episode is tantamount to treason.'

'To refuse my help?' she asked slowly. 'My help in unmask-
ing a spy? I do not understand. What does this mean?'

'It means just what I said,' Robespierre intervened coldly. 'That abominable English spy has fooled us all. You said yourself that 'tis a woman's wit that will bring that elusive adventurer to his knees one day. Why not yours?'

'I fear me, citizen Robespierre,' Theresia said after a while, 'that you overestimate the keenness of my wits.'

'Impossible!' he retorted dryly.

And St. Just, ever the echo of his friend's unspoken words, added with a great show of gallantry:

'The citoyenne Cabarrus, even from her prison in Bordeaux, succeeded in snaring our friend Tallien, and making him the slave of her beauty.'

'Then why not the Scarlet Pimpernel?' was Couthon's simple conclusion.

'The Scarlet Pimpernel!' Theresia exclaimed with a shrug of her handsome shoulders. 'The Scarlet Pimpernel, forsooth! Why meseems that no one knows who he is! Just now you all affirmed that he was a coal-heaver named Rateau.'

'Citizen Chauvelin knows who the Scarlet Pimpernel is,' Couthon went on deliberately. 'He will put you on the right track. All that we want is that he should be at your feet. It is so easy for the citoyenne Cabarrus to accomplish that.'

'But if you know who he is,' she urged, 'why do you need my help?'

'Because,' St. Just replied, 'the moment that he lands in France he sheds his identity, as a man would a coat. Here, there, everywhere – he is more elusive than a ghost, for a ghost is always the same, whilst the Scarlet Pimpernel is never twice alike. A coal-heaver one day; a prince of dandies the next. He has confederates everywhere: concierges, cabaret-keepers, soldiers, vagabonds. He has been a public letter-writer, a sergeant of the National Guard, a rogue, a thief! 'Tis only in England that he is always the same, and citizen Chauvelin can identify him there. 'Tis there that you can see him, citoyenne,

T—C

there that you can spread your nets for him; from thence that you can lure him to France in your train, as you lured citizen Tallien to obey your every whim in Bordeaux. Bring the Scarlet Pimpernel to your feet, here in Paris, citoyenne, and we will do the rest.'

When St. Just paused, Theresia waited awhile, her dark eyes fixed on the great man who had conceived this monstrous project. Theresia Cabarrus had in truth identified herself with the Revolutionary government. She had promised to marry Tallien, who outwardly at least was as bloodthirsty and ruthless as was Robespierre himself; but she was a woman and not a demon. She had refused to sell Bertrand Moncrif in order to pander to Tallien's fear of Robespierre. To entice a man – whoever he was – into making love to her, and then to betray him to his death, was in itself an abhorrent idea.

Womanlike, she tried to temporize.

She appeared puzzled; frowned. Then asked vaguely:

'Is it then that you wish me to go to England?'

St. Just nodded.

'But,' she continued, in the same indeterminate manner, 'meseems that you talk very glibly of my – what shall I say? – my proposed dalliance with the mysterious Englishman. Suppose he – he does not respond?'

'The citoyenne Cabarrus underrates her powers,' St. Just replied glibly.

'Theresia, I entreat!' Tallien put it dolefully.

He felt that the interview, from which he had hoped so much, was proving a failure – nay, worse! For he realized that Robespierre, thwarted in this desire, would bitterly resent Theresia's positive refusal to help him.

'Eh, what?' she answered. 'And is it you, citizen Tallien, who would push me into this adventure? I' faith, your trust in me is highly flattering! Have you not thought that in the process I might fall in love with the Scarlet Pimpernel myself? He

is young, they say; handsome, adventurous; and I am to try
to capture his fancy ... the butterfly is to dance around the
flame ... No, no! I am too much afraid that I may singe my
wings!'

'Does that mean,' Robespierre put in coldly, 'that you refuse
us your help, citoyenne Cabarrus?'

'Yes – I refuse,' she replied calmly. 'The project does not
please me, I confess –'

'Not even if we guaranteed immunity to your lover, Bertrand
Moncrif?'

She gave a slight shudder.

'I have no lover, except citizen Tallien,' she said steadily,
and placed her fingers, which had suddenly become ice-cold,
upon the clasped hands of her future lord. Then she rose,
thereby giving the signal for the breaking-up of the little
party.

Robespierre, taciturn and sullen, gave her one threatening
glance before he took his leave.

'You know, citoyenne,' he said coldly, 'that the nation has
means at its disposal for compelling its citizens to do their
duty.'

'Ah, bah!' retorted the fair Spaniard, shrugging her shoulders. 'I am not a citizen of France. And even your unerring
Public Prosecutor would find it difficult to frame an accusation
against me.'

Again she laughed, determined to appear gay and inconse-
quent through it all.

'Think how the accusation would sound, citizen Robespierre!' she went on mockingly. ' "The citoyenne Cabarrus, for
refusing to make amorous overtures to the mysterious Englishman known as the Scarlet Pimpernel, and for refusing to
administer a love-philtre to him as prepared by Mother Théot
at the bidding of citizen Robespierre" Confess! Confess!'
she added, and her rippling laugh had a genuine note of

merriment in it at last, 'that we none of us would survive such ridicule'.

Theresia Cabarrus was a clever woman, and by speaking the word 'ridicule', she had touched the one weak chink in the tyrant's armour. Tallien knew this well enough. He was on tenterhooks, longing to see the others depart so that he might throw himself once again at Theresia's feet and implore her to obey the despot's commands.

But Theresia appeared unwilling to give him such another chance. She professed intense fatigue, bade him 'good night' with such obvious finality, that he dared not outstay his welcome. A few minutes later they had all gone. The little procession was formed, with St. Just and Chauvelin supporting their palsied comrade, Robespierre detached and silent, and finally Tallien, whose last appealing look to his beloved would have melted a heart of stone.

11 | *Strange happenings*

Now the dingy little apartment in the Rue Villedot was silent and dark. The elegant little lamp with its rose-coloured shade was turned down in the withdrawing-room, leaving only a tiny glimmer of light, which failed to dispel the gloom around. The nocturnal visitors had departed more than a quarter of an hour ago; nevertheless the beautiful hostess had not yet gone to bed. Her eyes at intervals cast anxious looks upon the old-fashioned clock above the mantelpiece.

It struck half past two. Whereupon Theresia rose and went

out into the vestibule. Here a tallow candle flickered faintly in its pewter sconce and emitted an evil-smelling smoke, which rose in spirals to the blackened ceiling.

Theresia paused, glancing inquiringly down the narrow passage which gave access to the little kitchen beyond. Between the kitchen and the corner of the vestibule where she was standing, two doors gave on the passage: her bedroom, and that of her maid Pepita.

Theresia called:

'Pepita!'

But there came no answer. Pepita apparently had gone to bed, was fast asleep by now. But what had become of Bertrand?

Full of vague misgivings, Theresia picked up the candle and tiptoed down the passage. Outside Pepita's door she paused and listened.

'Pepita!' she called; and somehow the sound of her own voice added to her terror. She tried to open the door, but it was locked. Theresia knocked against the door, rattled the handle in its socket, called more loudly and more insistently, 'Pepita!' and, receiving no reply, fell, half-swooning with fear, against the partition wall, whilst the candle slipped out of her trembling grasp and fell with a clatter to the ground.

'Pepita!' she called again; and to her own ears her voice sounded hoarse and muffled. Straining her ears and holding her breath, she once more caught the sound of a smothered groan.

Pulling herself vigorously together, she began by groping for the candle which had dropped. Even as she stooped down for this she contrived to say in a moderately clear and firm voice:

'Courage, Pepita! I'll find the light and come back.' Then she added: 'Are you able to unlock the door?'

To this, however, she received no reply save another muffled groan.

Theresia now was on her hands and knees, groping for the candlestick. Her hands, as they wandered vaguely along the flagged floor, encountered a small object, which proved to be a key. In an instant she was on her feet again, her fingers running over the door until they encountered the keyhole. Into this she succeeded, after further groping, in inserting the key; it fitted, and turned the lock. She pushed open the door.

Pepita was reclining in an arm-chair, her hands tied behind her, a woollen shawl wound loosely around her mouth. In a distant corner of the room, a small oil lamp, turned very low, cast a glimmer of light upon the scene. For Theresia to run to the pinioned woman and undo the bonds that held her was but the work of a few seconds.

'Pepita!' she cried. 'What in heaven's name has happened?'

The woman seemed not much the worse for her enforced duress. She groaned, and indeed appeared more dazed then hurt. Theresia, impatient and excited, had to shake her vigorously by the shoulder before she was able to gather her scattered wits together.

'Where is M. Bertrand?' Theresia asked repeatedly.

At last Pepita was able to speak.

'In very truth, Madame,' she said slowly, 'I do not know.'

'How do you mean, you do not know?' Theresia queried, with a deepened frown.

'Just what I say, my pigeon,' Pepita retorted with marked acerbity. 'You ask me what has happened, and I say I do not know. You want to know what has become of M. Bertrand. Then go and look for yourself. When last I saw him, he was in the kitchen, unfit to move, the poor cabbage!'

'But, Pepita,' Theresia insisted, and stamped her foot with impatience, 'you must know how you came to be sitting here, pinioned and muffled. Who did it? Who has been here? God preserve the woman, will she never speak!'

Pepita by now had fully recovered her senses. She had struggled to her feet, and went to take up the lamp, then led the way towards the door, apparently intent on finding out for herself what had become of M. Bertrand and in no way sharing her mistress's unreasoning terror.

'M. Bertrand was sitting in the arm-chair in the kitchen,' she said simply. 'I was arranging a cushion for his head, to make him more comfortable, when suddenly a shawl was flung over my head without the slightest warning. And I had not the time to utter a scream before I was muffled up in the shawl. Then I was lifted off the ground as if I were a sack of feathers, and I just remember smelling something acrid which made my head spin round and round. But I remember nothing more after that until I heard voices in the vestibule when thy guests were going away. Then I heard thy voice and tried to make thee hear mine. And that is all!'

'When did that happen, Pepita?'

'Soon after the last of thy guests had arrived. I remember I looked at the clock. It must have been half an hour after midnight.'

When, the kitchen door being opened, that room was found to be empty, Theresia was no longer surprised. Somehow she had expected this. She knew that Bertrand would be gone. The windows of the kitchen gave on the wrought-iron balcony, as did all the other windows of the apartment. That those windows were unfastened, had only been pushed to from the outside, appeared to her as a matter of course. It was not Bertrand who had thrown the shawl over Pepita's head; therefore someone had come in from the outside and had kidnapped Bertrand – someone who was peculiarly bold and daring. He had not come in from the balcony and through the window, because the latter had been fastened as usual by Pepita much earlier in the evening. No! He had gone that way, taking Bertrand with him; but he must have entered the place in some other mysterious manner.

Whilst Pepita fumbled and grumbled, Theresia started on a tour of inspection. Still deeply puzzled, she was no longer afraid. With Pepita to speak to and the lamps all turned on, her habitual courage and self-possession had quickly returned to her.

Something was going on in her brain, certain theories, guesses, conjectures, which she was passionately eager to set at rest. Nor did it take her long. Candle in hand, she had gone round to explore. No sooner had she entered her own bedroom than the solution of the mystery lay revealed before her in a shutter, forced open from the outside, a broken pane of glass which had allowed a hand to creep in and turn the handle of the tall french window. It had been quickly and cleverly done; the splinters of glass had made no noise as they fell upon the carpet.

The frown of puzzlement deepened on Theresia Cabarrus's brow, and her mobile mouth with the perfectly arched if somewhat thin lips expressed a kind of feline anger, whilst the hand that held the pewter candlestick trembled perceptibly.

Pepita's astonishment expressed itself by sundry exclamations: 'Name of a name!' and 'Is it possible?'

The worthy old peasant absolutely refused to connect the departure of M. Bertrand with so obvious an attempt at housebreaking.

'M. Bertrand was determined to go, the poor cabbage!' she said decisively; 'since thou didst make him understand that his staying here was a danger to thee. He no doubt took an opportunity to slip out of the front door whilst thou wast engaged in conversation with that pack of murderers, whom may the good God punish one of these days!'

Theresia Cabarrus, wearied beyond endurance by all the events of this night, as well as her old servant's incessant gabble, finally sent her, still muttering and grumbling, to bed.

12 | *Chauvelin*

PEPITA went to bed. The clock of old St. Roch struck three.

Citoyenne Cabarrus, unable to sit still, wandered up and down the passage, in and out of the kitchen; in and out of her bedroom, and thence into the vestibule. Then back again.

She went to the front door and opened it. The quick cry which she gave was one of surprise rather than of fear. In her belated visitor she had recognized citizen Chauvelin; and somehow, by a vague process of reasoning his presence just at this moment seemed quite rational – in keeping with the unsolved mystery that was so baffling to the fair Theresia.

'May I come in, citoyenne?' Chauvelin said in a whisper. 'It is late, I know; but there is urgency.'

He was standing on the threshold, and she, a few paces away from him in the vestibule. The candle, which now burned low in its socket, was behind her. Its light touched with a weird, flickering glow the pale face of the once noted Terrorist, with its pale eyes and sharply hooked nose, which gave him the air of a gaunt bird of prey.

'It *is* late,' she murmured vaguely. 'What do you want?'

'Something has happened,' he replied, still speaking below his breath. 'Something which concerns you. And, before speaking of it to citizen Robespierre –'

At the dread name Theresia stepped farther back into the vestibule.

'Enter!' she said curtly.

She led the way into the withdrawing-room and turned up the wick of the lamp under its rosy shade.

'What is it?' she asked.

Before replying, Chauvelin's finger and thumb – thin and pointed like the talons of a vulture – went fumbling in the pocket of his waistcoat. From it he extracted a small piece of neatly folded paper.

'When we left your apartment, citoyenne – my friend St. Just and I supporting poor palsied Couthon, and Robespierre following close behind us – I spied this scrap of paper, which St. Just's careless foot had just kicked to one side when he was stepping across the threshold. Some unknown hand must have insinuated it underneath the door. Now, I never despise stray bits of paper. So, whilst the others were busy with their own affairs I, unseen by them, had already stooped and picked the paper up.'

Chauvelin slowly unfolded the note and began to read:

' "Bertrand Moncrif is a young fool, but he is too good to be the plaything of a sleek black pantheress, however beautiful she might be. So I am taking him away to England where, in the arms of his long-suffering and loyal sweetheart, he will soon forget the brief madness which so nearly landed him on the guillotine and made of him a tool to serve the selfish whims of Theresia Cabarrus." '

Theresia had listened to the brief epistle without displaying the slightest sign of emotion or surprise. Now, when Chauvelin had finished reading, and with his strange, dry smile handed her the tiny note, she took it and for a while contemplated it in silence.

'You know, of course, citoyenne,' Chauvelin said after a while, 'who the writer of this – shall we say? – impudent epistle happens to be?'

She nodded.

'The man,' he went on placidly, 'who goes by the name of the Scarlet Pimpernel. The impudent English adventurer whom citizen Robespierre has asked *you*, citoyenne, to lure into the net which we may spread for him.'

Still Theresia was silent.

'A while ago, citoyenne,' Chauvelin continued, 'in this very room, you refused to lend us a helping hand.'

Still no reply from Theresia. Chauvelin waited quite patiently.

Anon, a distant chime struck the quarter after three. Whereupon Chauvelin rose.

' I think we understand one another, citoyenne,' he said quietly, and with a sigh of complete satisfaction. 'It is late now. At what hour may I have the privilege of seeing you alone?'

'At three in the afternoon?' she replied tonelessly, like one speaking in a dream. 'Citizen Tallien is always at the Convention then, and my door will be denied to everybody else.'

'I'll be here at three o'clock,' was Chauvelin's final word.

He made her a deep bow and went out of the room.

13 | 'The Fisherman's Rest'

AND whilst the whole of Europe was in travail with the repercussion of the gigantic upheaval that was shaking France to its historic foundations, the last few years had seen but very little change in this little corner of England.

The Fisherman's Rest stood where it had done for two centuries. The oak rafters, black with age, the monumental hearth, the tables and high backed benches, seemed like mute testimonies to good order and to tradition.

Over in the kitchen yonder, Mistress Sally Waite, as she now was, still ruled with a firm hand, the weight of which,

even her husband, Master Harry Waite, had experienced more
than once.

And so it was still many a 'Ho, Sally! 'Ere, Sally! 'Ow
long'll you be with that there beer!' or 'Say, Sally! A cut of
your cheese and home-baked bread; and look sharp about it!'
that resounded from end to end of the long, low-raftered coffee-
room of *The Fisherman's Rest*, on this fine May day of the
year of grace 1794.

The while mine host, Master Jellyband, stood with stubby
legs firmly planted upon his own hearth, wherein, despite the
warmth of a glorious afternoon, a log fire blazed away merrily.
He was giving forth his views upon the political situation of
Europe generally with the self-satisfied assurance born of complete ignorance and true British insular prejudice.

Believe me, Mr. Jellyband was in no two minds about 'them
murderin' furriners over yonder' who had done away with their
King and Queen and all their nobility, and whom England
had at last decided to lick into shape.

'And not a moment too soon, hark'ee, Mr. 'Empseed,' he
went on sententiously. 'And if I 'ad my way, we should 'ave
punished 'em proper long before this – blown their bloomin'
Paris into smithereens, and carried off the pore Queen afore
those murderous villains 'ad 'er pretty 'ead off 'er shoulders!'

Mr. Hempseed, from his own privileged corner in the ingle-
nook, was not altogether prepared to admit that.

'I am not for interfering with other folks' ways,' he said,
raising his quaking treble so as to stem effectually the torrent
of Master Jellyband's eloquence. 'As the Scriptures say, Mr.
Jellyband: "'Ave no fellowship with the unfruitful work of
darkness." I don't 'old with interfering.'

But Mr. Jellyband was not thus lightly to be confounded in
his argument.

'All very fine, Mr. 'Empseed,' he said, 'and good enough
for them 'oo, like yourself, are willin' to side with them mur-

derin' reprobates. But I say that them as 'oo talk that way are not true Englishmen. And let me tell you, Mr. 'Empseed, that I'm prepared to back my opinions 'gainst any man as don't agree with me!'

Indeed, who was more qualified to pass an opinion on current events than the host of that much-frequented resort, seeing that the ladies and gentlemen of quality who came to England from over the water, so as to escape all them murtherin' reprobates in their own country, did most times halt at *The Fisherman's Rest* on their way to London or to Bath? And though Mr. Jellyband did not know a word of French, he nevertheless had mixed with all that nobility and gentry for over two years now, and had learned all that there was to know about the life over there, and about Mr. Pitt's intentions to put a stop to all those abominations.

Even now, a loud clatter on the cobble-stones outside, a jingle and a rattle, shouts, laughter, and bustle, announced the arrival of guests who were privileged to make as much noise as they pleased.

Mr. Jellyband ran to the door, shouted for Sally at the top of his voice, with a 'Here's my lord Hastings!' to add spur to Sally's hustle.

Three young gallants in travelling clothes, smart of appearance and debonair of mien, were ushering a party of strangers – three ladies and two men – in the hospitable porch of *The Fisherman's Rest*. The little party had walked across from the inner harbour, where the graceful masts of an elegant schooner lately arrived in port were seen gently swaying against the delicately coloured afternoon sky. Three or four sailors from the schooner were carrying luggage, which they deposited in the hall of the inn, then touched their forelocks in response to a pleasant smile and nod from the young lords.

'This way, my lord,' Master Jellyband reiterated with jovial obsequiousness. 'Everything is ready. This way! Hey, Sallee!'

he called again; and Sally, hot, excited, blushing, came tripping over from the kitchen, wiping her hot plump palms against her apron in anticipation of shaking hands with their lordships.

'Since Mr. Waite isn't anywhere about,' my lord Hastings said gaily, as he put a bold arm round Mistress Sally's dainty waist, 'I'll e'en have a kiss, my pretty one.'

'And I, too, by gad, for old sake's sake!' Lord Tony asserted, and planted a hearty kiss on Mistress Sally's dimpled cheek.

'At your service, my lords, at your service!' Master Jellyband rejoined, laughing. Then added more soberly: 'Now then, Sally, show the ladies up into the blue room, the while their lordships 'ave a first shake down in the coffee-room. This way, your lordships, this way!'

The strangers in the meanwhile had stood by, wide-eyed and somewhat bewildered in face of this exuberant hilarity which was so unlike what they had pictured to themselves of dull, fog-ridden England.

Lord Hastings, the youngest and merriest of the English party, guided the two Frenchmen towards the coffee-room.

Lord Antony Dewhurst and Sir Andrew Ffoulkes lingered a moment longer in the hall, in order to speak with the sailors who had brought the luggage along.

'Do you know aught of Sir Percy?' Lord Tony asked.

'No, my lord,' the sailor gave answer; 'not since he went ashore early this morning. 'Er ladyship was waitin' for 'im on the pier. Sir Percy just ran up the steps and then 'e shouted to us to get back quickly. "Tell their lordships," 'e says, "I'll meet them at The Rest." And then Sir Percy and 'er ladyship just walked off and we saw naun more of them.'

'That was many hours ago,' Sir Andrew Ffoulkes mused, with an inward smile.

' 'Twas just six o'clock when Sir Percy 'ad the boat lowered,' the sailor rejoined. 'And we rowed quick back after we landed 'im. But the *Day-Dream*, she 'ad to wait for the tide. We wurr a long while gettin' into port.'

Sir Andrew nodded.

'You don't know,' he said, 'if the skipper had any further orders?'

'I don't know, sir,' the man replied. 'But we mun be in readiness always. No one knows when Sir Percy may wish to set sail again.'

The two young men said nothing more, and presently the sailors touched their forelocks and went away. Lord Tony and Sir Andrew exchanged knowing smiles.

Far too impatient to wait until the tide allowed the *Day-Dream* to get into port, Sir Percy had been rowed ashore in the early dawn, and his beautiful Marguerite was there ready to receive him, to forget in the shelter of his arms the days of racking anxiety and of cruel terror for her beloved through which she had again and again been forced to pass.

As for the nineteen members of the League, they took it in turns to follow their leader where danger was thickest. It was a privilege eagerly sought, deserved by all, and accorded to those who were most highly trusted. It was invariably followed by a period of rest in happy England, with wife, friends, joy, and luxury. Sir Andrew Ffoulkes, Lord Antony Dewhurst, and my lord Hastings had been on the expedition which brought Mme de Serval with her three children and Bertrand Moncrif safely to England, after adventures more perilous, more reckless of danger, than most. Within a few hours they would be free to forget in the embrace of clinging arms every peril and every adventure save the eternal one of love, free to forswear everything outside that, save their veneration for their chief and their loyalty to his cause.

14 | *The castaway*

AN excellent dinner served by Mistress Sally and her attendant little wenches put everybody into rare good-humour. Madame de Serval even contrived to smile, her heart warmed by the genuine welcome, the rare gaiety that irradiated this fortunate corner of God's earth.

Joséphine and Jacques de Serval, whose enthusiasm for martyrdom had received so severe a check in the course of the Fraternal Supper in the Rue St. Honoré, had at first with the self-consciousness of youth adopted an attitude of obstinate and irreclaimable sorrow, until the antics of Master Harry Waite, pretty Sally's husband, brought laughter to their lips. My lord Hasting's comical attempts at speaking French, the droll mistakes he made, easily did the rest; and soon their lively, high-pitched Latin voices mingled with unimpaired gaiety with the more mellow sound of Anglo-Saxon tongues.

The only one who seemed quite unable to shake off his moroseness was Bertrand Moncrif. He sat next to Régine, silent, somewhat sullen, a look that seemed almost one of dull resentment lingering in his eyes.

It was when the merry meal was over and while Master Jellyband was going the round with a fine bottle of smuggled brandy, which the young gentlemen sipped with unmistakable relish, that a commotion arose outside the inn; whereupon Master Harry Waite ran out of the coffee-room in order to see what was amiss.

Nothing very much apparently. Waite came back after a moment or two and said that two sailors from the barque *Angela* were outside with a young French lad, who seemed more dead than alive, and whom it appears the barque had picked up just outside French waters, in an open boat, half perished with terror and inanition. As the lad spoke nothing but French, the sailors had brought him along to *The Fisherman's Rest*, thinking that maybe some of the quality would care to interrogate him.

At once Sir Andrew Ffoulkes, my lord Tony and Lord Hastings were on the qui vive. A lad in distress, coming from France, found alone in an open boat, suggested one of those tragedies in which the League of the Scarlet Pimpernel was wont to play a role.

'Let the lad be taken into the parlour, Jellyband,' Sir Andrew commanded. 'Then give him some of your smuggled brandy first, you old dog! then some wine and food.'

Jellyband, as usual, had already deputed his daughter to do the necessary, and in the hall there was Mistress Sally, capable and compassionate, supporting, almost carrying, a youth who in truth appeared scarce able to stand.

She led him gently into the small private parlour, where a cheerful log-fire was blazing, sat him down in an arm-chair beside the hearth, after which Master Jellyband himself poured half a glass of brandy down the poor lad's throat. This revived him a little, and he looked about him with huge, scared eyes.

'Sainte Mère de Dieu!' he murmured feebly. 'Where am I?'

'Never mind about that now, my lad,' replied Sir Andrew. 'You are among friends. That is enough. Have something to eat and drink now. Later we'll talk.'

He was eyeing the boy keenly. The lad spoke with a gentle, highly refined voice; his skin was delicate, and his face exquisitely beautiful; his hands, though covered with grime, and and his feet, encased in huge, coarse boots, were small and daintily shaped, like those of a woman. Already Sir Andrew had made up his mind that if the oilskin cap which sat so extraordinarily tight on the boy's head were to be removed, a wealth of long hair would certainly be revealed.

However, all these facts, which threw over the young stranger a further veil of mystery, could not in all humanity be investigated now. Sir Andrew Ffoulkes left the lad alone as soon as he appeared able to sit up and eat, and himself rejoined his friends in the coffee-room.

15 | *The nest*

No one knew of the little nest wherein Sir Percy Blakeney and his lady hid their happiness on those occasions when the Scarlet Pimpernel was only able to spend a few hours in England, and when a journey to their beautiful home in Richmond could not be thought of. The house lay about a mile and a half outside Dover, off the main road, perched up high on rising ground over a narrow lane. It had a small garden, which in May was ablaze with daffodils and bluebells, and in June with roses. Two faithful servants, a man and his wife, looked after the place, kept the nest cosy and warm whenever her ladyship, wearied of fashion, or else actually expecting Sir Percy, would come down from London.

A few days ago the weekly courier from France had brought her a line from Sir Percy, together with the promise that she should rest in his arms on the 1st of May.

She had stolen out at dawn to wait for him on the pier; and as soon as the May-day sun had dissipated the morning mist, her yearning eyes had spied the smart white gig which had put off from the *Day-Dream*, leaving the graceful ship to await the turn of the tide before putting into port.

Since then, every moment of the day had been one of rapture. The first sight of her husband in his huge caped coat, which seemed to add further inches to his great height, his call of triumph when he saw her, his arms outstretched, there, far away in the small boat, with a gesture of such infinite longing that for a second or two tears obscured Marguerite's vision. Then the drawing up of the boat against the landing-stage; Percy's spring ashore; his voice, his look; the strength of his arms; the ardour of his embrace.

After that, breakfast in the low, raftered room – the hot, savoury milk, the home-baked bread, the home-churned butter. Then the long, delicious, intimate talk. Blakeney kept nothing secret from his wife; and what he did not tell her, that she easily guessed. But it was from the members of the League that she learned all there was to know of heroism and selflessness in the perilous adventures through which her husband passed with so lighthearted a gaiety.

'You should see me as an asthmatic reprobate, m'dear,' he would say, with his infectious laugh. 'And hear that cough! Lud love you, but I am mightily proud of that cough! Poor old Rateau does not do it better himself; and he is genuinely asthmatic.'

He gave her an example of his prowess; but she would not allow him to go on.

'Rateau was a real find,' he went on more seriously; 'because he is three parts an imbecile and as obedient as a dog. When some of those devils are on my track, lo! the real Rateau appears and yours truly vanishes where no one can find him! They have become so confused now between Rateau the coal-heaver, the mysterious Scarlet Pimpernel, and the problematic English milord, that all three of these personalities can appear before their eyes and they will let them all escape! I assure you that the confusion between the Scarlet Pimpernel who was in the ante-chamber of Mother Théot on that fateful afternoon, and again at the Fraternal Supper in the Rue St. Honoré, and the real Rateau who was at Mother Théot's while that same exciting supper party was going on, was so great that not one of those murdering reprobates could trust his own eyes and ears, and we got away as easily as rabbits out of a torn net.'

Thus did he explain and laugh over the perilous adventure where he had faced a howling mob disguised as Rateau the coalheaver, and with almost superhuman pluck and boldness had dragged Mme. de Serval and her children into the derelict house, one of the League's headquarters. That is how he charac-terized the extraordinary feat of audacity when, in order to give his gallant lieutenants time to smuggle the unfortunates out of the house through a back and secret way, he showed him-self on the balcony above the multitude, and hurled dummy figures into the brazier below.

Then came the story of Bertrand Moncrif, snatched half-unconscious out of the apartment of fair Theresia Cabarrus, whilst Robespierre himself sat not six yards away, with only the thickness of a wall between him and his arch enemy.

'How the woman must hate you!' Marguerite murmured, with a slight shudder of acute anxiety which she did her best to conceal. 'There are things that a woman like the Cabarrus will never forgive. Whether she cares for Bertrand Moncrif or no, her vanity will suffer intensely, and she will never for-give you for taking him out of her clutches.'

He laughed.

'Lud, m'dear!' he said lightly. 'If we were to take heed of all the people who hate us we should spend our lives pondering rather than doing.'

It was some hours later on that same glorious day that Sir Percy and Marguerite sat in the deep window-embrasure of the tiny living-room.

Then it was that suddenly a man's voice, hoarse but distinct, broke in upon the perfect peace around. What it said could not at first be gathered. Marguerite whispered:

'Listen!'

The man's voice had been answered by a woman's, raised as if in defiance that seemed both pitiful and futile.

'You cannot harm me now. I am in England!'

Marguerite leaned out of the window, tried to peer into the darkness which was fast gathering over the lane. The voices had come from there: first the man's, then the woman's, and now the man's again; both speaking in French, the woman obviously terrified and pleading, the man harsh and commanding. Now it was raised again, more incisive and distinct than before, and Marguerite had in truth some difficulty in repressing the cry that rose to her lips. She had recognized the man's voice.

'Chauvelin!' she murmured.

'Aye, in England, citoyenne!' that ominous voice went on dryly. 'But the arm of justice is long. And remember that you are not the first who has tried – unsuccessfully, let me tell you! – to evade punishment by flying to the enemies of France. Wherever you may hide, I will know how to find you. Have I not found you here, now? – and you but a few hours in Dover!'

'But you cannot touch me!' the woman protested with the courage of one in despair.

The man laughed.

'Are you really simple enough, citoyenne,' he said, 'to be convinced of that?'

This sarcastic retort was followed by a moment or two of silence, then by a woman's cry; and in an instant Sir Percy was on his feet and out of the house.

It was close beside the gate that a human-looking bundle lay huddled, when Sir Percy came upon the scene, even whilst, some fifty yards away at the sharp bend of the lane, a man could be seen walking rapidly away, his pace well-nigh at a run. Sir Percy's instinct was for giving chase, but the huddled-up figure put out a pair of arms and clung to him so desperately, with smothered cries of: 'For pity's sake, don't leave me!' that it would have been inhuman to go. And so he bent down, raised the human bundle from the ground, and carried it bodily up into the house.

The human bundle looked very pathetic lying there upon the window seat, propped up with cushions. It appeared to be a youth, dressed in rough fisherman's clothes and with a cap that fitted tightly round the head; but with hands delicate as a woman's and a face of exquisite beauty.

Without another word, Marguerite quietly took hold of the cap and gently removed it. A wealth of blue-black hair fell like a cascade over the recumbent shoulders. 'I thought as much!' Sir Percy remarked quietly, even whilst the stranger, apparently terrified, jumped up and burst into tears, moaning piteously.

The stranger, with a wry little smile, took the handkerchief which Lady Blakeney was holding out to her and proceeded to dry her tears.

'I am an imposter, I know,' she said, with lips that quivered like those of a child in grief. 'But if you only knew . . . !'

She sat bolt upright now, squeezing and twirling the wet handkerchief between her fingers.

'Some kind English gentlemen were good to me, down in the town,' she went on more glibly. 'They gave me food and shelter, and I was left alone to rest. But I felt stifled in the narrow room. I could hear everyone talking and laughing, and the evening air was so beautiful. So I ventured out. I only meant to breathe a little fresh air; but it was all so lovely, so peaceful . . . here in England . . . so different to . . .'

She shuddered a little and looked as if she was going to cry again. But Marguerite interposed gently:

'So you prolonged your walk, and found this lane?'

'Yes. I prolonged my walk,' the woman replied. 'I did not notice that the road had become lonely. Then suddenly I realized that I was being followed, and I ran. Mon Dieu, how I ran! Whither, I knew not! I just felt that something horrible was at my heels!'

Marguerite gave her trembling hands an encouraging pat.

'It was lucky,' she said gently, 'that you found your way here.'

'I had seen the light,' the woman continued more calmly. 'And I believe that at the back of my mind there was the instinct to run for shelter. Then suddenly my foot knocked against a stone, and I fell. I tried to raise myself quickly, but I had not the time, for the next moment I felt a hand on my shoulder, and a voice – oh, a voice I dread, citoyenne! – called to me by name.'

'The voice of citizen Chauvelin?' Marguerite asked simply.

The woman looked up quickly.

'You knew – ?' she murmured.

'I knew his voice.'

'But you know him?' the other insisted.

'I know him – yes,' Marguerite replied. 'I am a compatriot of yours. Before I married, I was Marguerite St. Just.'

'St. Just?'

'We are cousins, my brother and I, of the young deputy, the friend of Robespierre.'

'God help you!' the woman murmured.

'He has done so already, by bringing us both to England. My brother is married, and I am Lady Blakeney now. You too will feel happy and safe now that you are here.'

'Happy?' the woman ejaculated, with a piteous sob. 'And safe? Mon Dieu, if only I could think of it!'

'But what have you to fear? Chauvelin may have retained

some semblance of power over in France. He has none over
here.'

'He hates me!' the other murmured. 'Oh, how he hates me!'

'Why?'

The stranger made no immediate reply. Then after a while
she went on, with seeming irrelevance:

'It all began so foolishly! . . . mon Dieu, how foolishly! And
I really meant nothing treacherous to my own country – nothing
unpatriotic, quoi?' She suddenly seized Marguerite's two hands
and exclaimed with childlike enthusiasm: 'You have heard of
the Scarlet Pimpernel, have you not?'

'Yes,' Marguerite replied. 'I have heard of him.'

'You know then that he is the finest, bravest, most wonderful man in all the world?'

'Yes, I know that,' Marguerite assented with a smile.

'Of course, in France they hate him. Naturally! He is the
enemy of the republic, quoi? He is against all those massacres,
the persecution of the innocent. He saves them and helps them
when he can. So they hate him. Naturally.'

'Naturally!'

'But I have always admired him,' the woman continued, enthusiasm glowing in her dark eyes. 'Always; always! Ever since
I heard what he had done, and how he saved the Comte de
Tournay and Juliette Marny, and Esther Vincent, and – and
countless others. Oh, I knew about them all! For I knew
Chauvelin well, and one or two of the men on the Committee
of Public Safety quite intimately, and I used to worm out of
them all the true facts about the Scarlet Pimpernel. Can you
wonder that with my whole soul I admired him? I worshipped
him! So now you understand perhaps why Chauvelin hates
me!'

'You must have been rather indiscreet,' Marguerite remarked
with a smile.

'I was, I suppose. And Chauvelin is so vindictive. He hates

the Scarlet Pimpernel. Out of a few words, foolishly spoken perhaps, he has made out a case against me. A friend gave me warning. My name was already in the hands of Foucquier-Tinville. You know what that means! Arrest! Judgment! Then the guillotine! Oh, mon Dieu. I fled out of Paris. A faithful servant accompanied me. We reached Boulogne. I was so weak, so ill, so wretched. I hardly lived. We had no passports, no papers – nothing. We had to hide – in barns ... in pig-stys ... anywhere! But we reached Boulogne at last ... I had some money, fortunately. We bribed a fisherman to let us have his boat. Only a small boat – imagine! A rowing-boat! And François and I alone in it. But it meant our lives if we didn't go; and perhaps it meant our lives if we went! A rowing-boat on the great, big sea! ... Fortunately the weather was fine, and François said that surely we would meet an English vessel which would pick us up. I was so tired. It is possible that I slept. Then suddenly something woke me. I had heard a cry. I knew I had heard a cry, and then a splash – an awful splash! I was wet through. One oar hung in the rowlock; the other had gone. And François was not there. I was all alone.'

She spoke in hard, jerky sentences, as if every word hurt her physically, as she uttered it. Now and again she looked up, not at Marguerite always, rather at Sir Percy. Her glowing, tear-wet eyes fastened themselves on him from time to time with an appealing or a defiant gaze. He appeared silent and sympathetic, and his glance rested on her the whole while with an expression of detached if kindly interest, as if he did not quite understand everything that she said. Marguerite as usual was full of tenderness and compassion.

'How terribly you must have suffered!' she said gently. 'But what happened after that?'

'I remember nothing after ... after that awful cry ... and the splash! I suppose my poor François fainted or fell asleep ... and that he fell into the water. I never saw him again ...

And I remember nothing until – until I found myself on board a ship with a lot of rough sailors around me, who seemed very kind ... They brought me ashore and took me to a nice warm place, where some English gentlemen took compassion on me. And ... and ... I have already told you the rest.'

She struggled to her feet, rose with obvious reluctance.

'The inn where I was,' she said, 'it is not far?'

'But you cannot go out alone,' Marguerite rejoined. 'You do not even know the way!'

'Ah, no! But perhaps your servant could accompany me ... only as far as the town ... after that, I can ask the way ... I should no longer be frightened.'

'You speak English then, Madame?'

'Oh, yes! My father was a diplomat. He was in England once for four years. I learned a little English. I have not forgotten it.'

'One of the servants shall certainly go with you. The inn you speak of must be *The Fisherman's Rest*, since you found English gentlemen there.'

'If Madame will allow me?' Sir Percy broke in, for the first time since the stranger had embarked upon her narrative.

'You milord!' she exclaimed. 'Oh no! I would be ashamed –'

She paused, and looked down in confusion on her extra-ordinary attire.

'I had forgotten,' she murmured tearfully. 'François made me put on these awful clothes when we left Paris.'

'Then I must lend you a cloak for tonight,' Marguerite inter-posed with a smile. 'But you need not mind your clothes, Madame. On this coast our people are used to seeing unfor-tunate fugitives landing in every sort of guise. Tomorrow we must find you something wherein to travel to London.'

'To London?' the stranger said with some eagerness. 'Yes! I would wish to go to London.'

'It will be quite easy. Mme. de Serval, with her son and

two daughters and another friend, is travelling by the coach tomorrow. You could join them, I am sure. Then you would not be alone. You have money, Madame?' Marguerite concluded, with practical solicitude.

'Oh yes!' the other replied. 'I have plenty for present needs. I was able to collect a little – and I have not lost it. I am not dependent,' she added, with a smile of gratitude. 'And as soon as I have found my husband –'

'Your husband?' Marguerite exclaimed.

'M. le Marquis de Fontenay,' the other answered simply. 'Perhaps you know him. You have seen him . . . in London? . . . Non?'

Marguerite shook her head.

'Not to my knowledge.'

'He left me – two years ago . . . cruelly . . . emigrated to England . . . and I was left all alone in the world . . . He saved his own life by running away from France; but I – I could not go just then . . . and so . . .'

Marguerite said gently. 'I have friends in London who are in touch with most of the émigrés here. We will see what can be done. It will not be difficult, methinks, to find M. de Fontenay.'

'You are an angel, milady!' the stranger exclaimed. Then she once more mopped her eyes, picked up her cap and hastily hid the wealth of her hair beneath it. After which, she turned to Sir Percy.

'I am ready, milord,' she said. 'I have intruded far too long as it is upon your privacy . . .'

She wrapped herself up in a cloak which, at Lady Blakeney's bidding, one of the servants had brought her, and a moment or two later the stranger and Sir Percy were out of the house, whilst Marguerite remained for a while in the porch, listening to their retreating footsteps.

There was a frown of puzzlement between her brows, a look of troubled anxiety in her eyes. Somehow, the brief sojourn of

that strange and beautiful woman in her house had filled her
soul with a vague feeling of dread, which she tried vainly to
combat.

16 | *A lover of sport*

FOR the first five minutes, Sir Percy Blakeney and Madame de
Fontenay walked side by side in silence. Then she spoke.

'You are silent, milord?' she queried, speaking in perfect
English.

'I was thinking,' he replied curtly.

'What?'

'That a remarkably fine actress is lost in the fashionable
Theresia Cabarrus.'

'Madame de Fontenay, I pray you, milord,' she retorted
dryly.

'Theresia Cabarrus nevertheless. Madame Tallien probably
tomorrow: for Madame divorced that weak-kneed marquis as
soon as the law "contre les émigrés" allowed her to regain her
freedom.'

'You seem very well informed, milord.'

'Almost as well as Madame herself,' he riposted with a
pleasant laugh.

'Then you do not believe my story?'

'Not one word of it!' he replied.

'Strange!' she mused. 'For every word of it is true. Of course,
I did not tell all,' she went on. 'I could not. My lady would not
understand. She has become — what shall I say? — very English.

Marguerite St. Just would understand . . . Lady Blakeney – no?'

'What would Lady Blakeney not understand?'

'Eh bien! About Bertrand Moncrif.'

'Ah?'

'You think I did harm to the boy . . . I know . . . you took him away from me . . . You! The Scarlet Pimpernel! . . . You see, I know everything! Chauvelin told me . . .'

'And guided you most dexterously to my door,' he concluded with a pleasant laugh. 'There to enact a delicious comedy of gruff-voiced bully and pathetic victim of a merciless persecution. It was all excellently done. Allow me to offer you my sincere congratulations!'

'You think that I am here in order to spy upon you?'

'Oh!' he riposted lightly, 'how could I be so presumptuous as to suppose that the beautiful Cabarrus would bestow attention on so unworthy an object as I?'

' 'Tis you now, milord,' she rejoined dryly, 'who choose to play a role. A truce on it, I pray you; and rather tell me what you mean to do.'

To this query he gave no reply, and his silence appeared to grate on Theresia's nerves, for she went on harshly:

'You will betray me to the police, of course. And as I am here without papers –'

'Oh!' he said, with his quiet little laugh, 'why should you think I would do anything so unchivalrous?'

'Unchivalrous?' she retorted. 'I suppose, here in England, it would be called an act of patriotism or self-preservation . . . like fighting an enemy . . . or denouncing a spy –'

She paused for a moment or two, and as he once more took refuge in silence, she resumed with sudden, moving passion:

'So it is to be a betrayal after all! The selling of an unfortunate woman to her bitterest enemy! Oh, what wrong have I ever done you, that you should persecute me thus?'

'Persecute you?' he exclaimed. 'Pardi, Madame; but this is

a subtle joke which by your leave my dull wits are unable to fathom.'

'It is no joke, milord,' she rejoined earnestly. 'Will you let me explain? For indeed it seems to me that we are at cross purposes, you and I. That boy,' she went on quite gently, 'Bertrand Moncrif, was just a young fool. But I liked him, and I could see the abyss to which his folly was tending. There was never anything but friendship between us; but I knew that sooner or later he would run his head into a noose, and then what good would his pasty-faced sweetheart have been to him? Whilst I – I had friends, influence – quoi? And I liked the boy; I was sorry for him.

'Then the catastrophe came . . . the other night. There was what those ferocious beasts over in Paris were pleased to call a Fraternal Supper. Bertrand Moncrif was there. Like a young fool, he started to vilify Robespierre. I don't know just what happened, for I wasn't there; but he came to my apartment – at midnight – dishevelled – his clothes torn – more dead than alive. I gave him shelter; I tended him. Yes, I! – even whilst Robespierre and his friends were in my house, and I risked my life every moment that Bertrand was under my roof! Chauvelin suspected something then. At which precise moment you came and took Bertrand away, I know not. But Chauvelin knew. Then, after the others had left, he came back, accused me of having harboured not only Bertrand, but the Scarlet Pimpernel himself! – swore that I was in league with the English spies and had arranged with them to smuggle my lover out of my house.

'Then he went away. He did not threaten. But from his look I knew that I was doomed. Luckily I had François. We packed up my few belongings then and there. I left my woman Pepita in charge, and I fled. As for the rest, I swear to you that it all happened just as I told it to milady. You say you do not believe me. Very well! Will you then take me away from this sheltered land, which I have reached after terrible sufferings? Will you send me back to France, and drive me to the arms of a man who but waits to throw me into the tumbril with the next batch of victims for the guillotine? You have the power to do it, of course. You can do with me what you will, of course. But if you do *that*, milord, my blood will stain your hands for ever; and all the good you and your League have ever done in the cause of humanity will be wiped out by this execrable crime.'

Sir Percy spoke to her quite gently.

'Believe me, dear lady,' he said, 'that I had no thought of wronging you when I owned to disbelieving your story.'

'Had you known me better, milord –' she began.

'Ah, that is just it!' he rejoined quaintly. 'I did not know you, Madame. And now, meseems, that Fate has intervened, and that I shall never have the chance of knowing you.'

'How is that?' she asked.

'Oh!' he retorted simply. 'You are staying in England, you tell me.'

'If you will deign to grant me leave,' she said, with gentle submission.

'It is not in my power to grant or to refuse.'

'You will not betray me – to the police?'

'I have never betrayed a woman in my life.'

'Or to Lady Blakeney?'

He made no answer.

'Or to Lady Blakeney?' she insisted.

Then, as he still gave no answer, she began to plead with passionate earnestness.

'What could she gain – or you – by her knowing that I am that unfortunate, homeless waif, without kindred and without friends, Theresia Cabarrus. Do not tell Lady Blakeney, milord! On my knees I entreat you, do not tell her! Oh, give me a chance to be happy! Give me – a chance – to be happy!'

Suddenly, without any warning, he threw back his head and laughed.

'By Gad!' he exclaimed. 'But you are a clever woman!'

'Milord!' she protested, indignant.

'Nay : you need have no fear. I'll not betray you.'

She frowned, really puzzled this time.

'I do not understand,' she murmured.

'Let us get back to *The Fisherman's Rest,*' he retorted. 'Shall we?'

'Milord,' she insisted, 'will you explain?'

'There is nothing to explain, dear lady. You have asked me – nay challenged me – not to betray you to anyone, not even to Lady Blakeney. Very well! I accept your challenge. That is all.'

'You will not tell anyone – anyone, mind you! – that Mme. de Fontenay and Theresia Cabarrus are one and the same?'

'You have my word for that.'

'Very well then, milord,' she rejoined. 'Since I am allowed to go to London, we shall meet there, I hope.'

'Scarcely, dear lady,' he replied, 'since I go to France tomorrow.'

'You go to France tomorrow, milord?' she asked.

'As I had the honour to tell you, I go to France tomorrow, and I leave you a free hand to come and go as you please.'

'If you go, I shall go too.'

'I am sure you will, dear lady,' he retorted with a smile. 'So there really is no reason why we should linger here. Our mutual friend M. Chauvelin must be impatient to hear the result of this interview.'

She gave a cry of horror and indignation.

'Oh! You – you still think *that* of *me*?'

He stood there, smiling, looking down on her with that half amused, lazy glance of his. She turned abruptly, and burying her face in her hands, sobbed as if her heart would break. Sir

Percy waited quietly for a moment or two, then he said gently:

'Madame, I entreat you to compose yourself and to dry your tears. I pray you to understand that when a man holds human lives in his hands, when he is responsible for the life and safety of those who trust in him, he must be doubly cautious and in his turn trust no one. You have said yourself that now at last in this game of life and death, which I and my friends have played so successfully these last three years, I hold the losing cards. Then must I watch every trick all the more closely, for a sound player can win through the mistakes of his opponent, even if he hold a losing hand.'

But she refused to be comforted.

'You will never know, milord – never – how deeply you have wounded me,' she said through her tears. 'And I, who for months past – ever since I knew! – have dreamed of seeing the Scarlet Pimpernel one day! He was the hero of my dreams, the man who stood alone in the mass of self-seeking, vengeful, cowardly humanity as the personification of all that was fine and chivalrous. I longed to see him – just once – to hold his hand – to look into his eyes – and feel a better woman for the experience. Chance brings me face to face with the hero of my dreams, and he looks on me as that vilest thing on earth: a spy! – a woman who would lie to a man first and send him afterwards to his death!'

Sir Percy listened – quite quietly, as was his wont – to her strange words. She dried her eyes and after a moment or two, of her own accord, she started once more on her way.

Nor did they speak again with one another until they were under the porch of *The Fisherman's Rest*. Then Theresia stopped, and with a perfectly simple gesture she held out her hand to Sir Percy.

'We may never meet again on this earth, milord,' she said quietly. 'Indeed, I shall pray to le bon Dieu to keep me clear of your path.'

T—D

'I very much doubt, dear lady,' he said, 'that you will be in earnest when you utter that prayer!'

'You choose to suspect me, milord; and I'll no longer try to combat your mistrust. But to one more word you must listen: Remember the fable of the lion and the mouse. The invincible Scarlet Pimpernel might one day need the help of Theresia Cabarrus. I would wish you to believe that you can always count on it.'

She extended her hand to him, and he took it, the while his mocking glance challenged her earnest one. After a moment or two he stooped and kissed her finger-tips.

'Let me rather put it differently, dear lady,' he said. 'One day the exquisite Theresia Cabarrus – the Egeria of the Terrorists, the fiancée of the Great Tallien – might need the help of the League of the Scarlet Pimpernel.'

'I would sooner die than seek your help, milord,' she protested earnestly.

'Here in Dover, perhaps ... but in France? ... And you said you were going back to France, in spite of Chauvelin and his pale eyes, and his suspicions of you.'

'Since you think so ill of me,' she retorted, 'why should you offer me your help?'

'Because,' he replied lightly, 'with the exception of my friend Chauvelin, I have never had so amusing an enemy; and it would afford me intense satisfaction to render you a signal service.'

'You mean that you would risk your life to save mine?'

'No. I should not risk my life, dear lady,' he said with his puzzling smile. 'But I should – God help me! – do my best, if the need arose, to save yours.'

After which, with another ceremonious bow, he took final leave of her, and she was left standing there, looking after his tall, retreating figure until the turn of the street hid him from view.

For a long while she remained standing in the porch.

Well! he had defied and insulted her. The letter which he left for her after he had smuggled Bertrand Moncrif out of her apartment, rankled and stung her pride as nothing had ever done before. Therefore the man must be punished, and in a manner that would leave no doubt in his mind as to whence came the blow that struck him. But it was all going to be very much more difficult than the beautiful Theresia Cabarrus had allowed herself to believe.

17 | *Reunion*

IT was a thoughtful Theresia who turned into the narrow hall of *The Fisherman's Rest* a few moments later. The inn, when she left it earlier in the evening, had still been all animation and bustle consequent on the arrival of their lordships with the party of ladies and gentlemen over from France, and the excitement of making all these grand folk comfortable for the night.

The young English gallants had gone, either to friends in the neighbourhood or – in the case of Sir Andrew Ffoulkes and Lord Antony Dewhurst – ridden away in the early part of the evening, so as to reach Ashford mayhap or Maidstone before nightfall, and thus lessen the distance which still separated them from the loved ones at home.

Theresia slipped noiselessly past the glass door. Straight in front of her a second passage ran at right angles; two or three steps led up to it. She tiptoed up these, and then looked about her, trying to reconstruct in her mind the disposition of the various rooms. On her left a glass partition divided the passage from the small parlour wherein she had found shelter on her arrival. On her right the passage obviously led to the kitchen, for much noise of crockery and shrill feminine voices and laughter came from there.

For a moment Theresia hesitated. Her original intention had been to find Mistress Waite and see if a bed for the night were still available; but a slight noise or movement issuing from the parlour caused her to turn. She peeped through the glass partition. The room was dimly lighted by a small oil-lamp which hung from the ceiling. A fire still smouldered in the hearth, and beside it, sitting on a low stool staring into the embers, his hands held between his knees, was Bertrand Moncrif.

Theresia Cabarrus had some difficulty in smothering the cry of surprise which had risen to her throat. She opened the door quite noiselessly and slipped into the room. Bertrand had not moved. Apparently he had not heard. Theresia drew the curtains together that hung in front of the glass partition, and thus made sure that intruding eyes could not catch her unawares. Then she murmured softly:

'Bertrand!'

He woke as from a dream, looked up and saw her. A hoarse cry escaped him, and the next moment he was down on his knees at her feet, his arms around her, his face buried in the folds of her mantle.   .

After a while he rose, and she allowed him to lead her to an arm-chair by the hearth.

She insisted on hearing every detail of his escape out of Paris and out of France, under the protection of the League of the Scarlet Pimpernel. In truth, he did not know who his rescuer was. He remembered but little of that awful night when, after the terrible doings at the Fraternal Supper, he had sought refuge in her apartment.

He had resolved to go as soon as he was able to stand – resolved if need be to give himself up at the nearest Poste de Section, when in a semi-conscious state he became aware that someone was in the room with him. He had not the time or the power to rouse himself and to look about, when a cloth was thrown over his face and he felt himself lifted off the chair bodily and carried away by powerful arms.

After that, a great deal had happened – it all seemed indeed like a dream. At one time he was with Régine de Serval in a coach; at others with her brother Jacques, in a hut at night, lying on straw, trying to get some sleep, and tortured with thoughts of Theresia and fear for her safety. Régine was constantly with him. She did her best to comfort him, would try to while away the weary hours in the coach or in various hiding-places by holding his hand and talking of the future – the happy future in England, when they would have a home of their own, secure from the terrors of the past two years, peaceful in complete oblivion of the cruel past.

Theresia listened to the tale, for the most part in silence. She did ask one or two questions, but these chiefly on the subject of his rescuer: Had he seen him? Had he seen any of the English gentlemen who effected his escape?

Oh, yes! Bertrand saw a good deal of the three or four young gallants who accompanied him and the party all the way from Paris. He only saw the last of them here, in this inn, a few hours ago. One of them gave him some money to enable him to reach London in comfort. They were very kind, entirely unselfish.

But the Scarlet Pimpernel himself, Theresia insisted, trying to conceal her impatience under a veneer of tender solicitude – had Bertrand seen him?

'No!' Bertrand replied. 'I never once set eyes on him, though it was he undoubtedly who dragged me helpless out of your apartment. The others spoke of him – always as "the chief". They seem to reverence him. He must be fine and brave. Régine

and her mother and the two young ones have learned to worship him. Small wonder! seeing what he did for them at that
awful Fraternal Supper.'

'What did he do?' Theresia queried.

And the story had to be told by Bertrand, just as he had had
it straight from Régine. The asthmatic coalheaver – the
quarrel – Robespierre's arrival on the scene – the shouts – the
mob. The terror of that awful giant who had dragged them into
the empty house, and there left them in the care of others scarce
less brave than himself. Then the disguises – the wanderings
through the streets – the deathly anxiety at the gates of the
city – the final escape in a laundry cart.

'On my knees will I pay homage to him,' Bertrand concluded
fervently; 'since he brought you to my arms!'

She had him by the shoulders, held him from her at arm's
length, whilst she looked – inquiringly, slightly mocking – into
his eyes.

'Brought me to your arms, Bertrand?' she said slowly. 'What
do you mean?'

'You are here, Theresia,' he riposted. 'Safe in England . . .
through the agency of the Scarlet Pimpernel.'

She gave a hard, mirthless laugh.

'Aye!' she said dryly; 'through his agency. But not as you
imagine, Bertrand.'

'What do you mean?'

'The Scarlet Pimpernel, my friend, after he had dragged you
away from the shelter which you had found under my roof,
sent an anonymous denunciation of me to the nearest Poste de
Section, as having harboured the traitor Moncrif and conspiring with him to assassinate Robespierre whilst the latter was in
my apartment.'

Bertrand uttered a cry of horror.

'Impossible!' he exclaimed.

'The chief Commissary of the Section,' she went on glibly,

earnestly – never taking her eyes off his, 'at risk of his life, gave me warning. Aided by him and a faithful servant, I contrived to escape – out of Paris first, then across country in the midst of unspeakable misery, and finally out of the country in an open boat, until I was picked up by a chance vessel and brought to this inn more dead than alive.'

She fell back against the cushion of the chair, her body shaken with sobs. After a while she became more calm, contrived to smile through her tears.

'You see, Bertrand, that your gallant Scarlet Pimpernel is as merciless in hate as he is selfless in love.'

'But why?' the young man ejaculated vehemently. 'Why?'

'Why should he hate me?' she rejoined with a pathetic little sigh and a shrug of the shoulders. 'Of course, he does not know that of late – ever since I have gained the regard of citizen Tallien – my life has been devoted to intervening on behalf of the innocent victims of our revolution. He has forgotten what I did in Bordeaux, and how I risked my life there, and did so daily in Paris for the sake of those whom he himself befriends. It may all be a question of misunderstanding,' she added, with gentle resignation, 'but 'tis one that well-nigh did cost me my life.'

Theresia glanced up at the clock. It was close upon ten. Confused, adorable, she jumped to her feet.

She would arrange with the landlord's daughter, she said, about a bed for herself, as she was very tired. What did he mean to do?

'Spend the night in this room,' he replied, 'if mine host will let me.'

Bertrand drew a deep sigh, partly of happiness, partly of utter weariness. He was more tired than he knew. She had promised to come back and say good night . . . in a few minutes . . . But the minutes seemed leaden-footed now . . . and he was half-dead with fatigue. He threw himself down on the hard, uncomfortable horsehair sofa, whereon he hoped to pass the night if the landlord would let him, and glanced up at the clock. Only three minutes since she had gone . . . of course she would not be long . . . only a few more minutes . . . a very few . . . He closed his eyes, for the lids felt heavy . . . of a surety he would hear her come . . .

18 | *Night and morning*

THERESIA waited for a moment or two at the turn of the passage, until her keen ear had told her that Bertrand was no longer on the watch and had closed the door behind him. Then she retraced her steps.

She found her way to the front door; it was still on the latch. She opened it and peered out into the night. She was on the point of stepping out of the porch, when a familiar voice hailed her softly by name:

'Citoyenne Cabarrus!'

A man, dressed in dark clothes, with high boots and sugar-loaf hat, came out from the dark angle behind the porch.

'Not here!' Theresia whispered eagerly. 'Out on the quay. Wait for me there, my little Chauvelin. I'll be with you anon. I have so much to tell you!'

Silently, he did as she desired. She waited for a moment in the porch, watching the meagre figure in the dark cloak making its way across to the quay, then walking rapidly in the direction of the Pent. The groups of passers-by had dwindled down to an occasional couple strolling homewards, or half a dozen sailors lolling down the quays arm in arm, on their way back to their ship, obstructing the road, yelling and singing the refrain of the newest ribald song; or perhaps a belated pedlar, weary of an unprofitable beat, wending his way dejectedly home.

One of these poor wretches – a cripple with a wooden leg and bent nearly double with the heavy load on his back – paused for a moment beside the porch, held out a grimy hand to Theresia, with a pitiable cry.

'Of your charity, kind sir! Buy a little something from a pore ole man, to buy a bit of bread!'

He looked utterly woebegone, with lank grey hair blown about by the breeze and a colourless face covered with sweat, that shone like painted metal in the moonlight.

Theresia – a little frightened, and not at all charitably inclined at this hour – turned hastily away and went back into the house, whither the cripple's vigorous curses followed her.

With infinite precaution, Theresia peeped into the room where she had left Bertrand. She saw him lying on the sofa, fast asleep.

On the table in the middle of the room there was an old inkhorn, a pen, and a few loose sheets of paper. Noiseless as a mouse, Theresia slipped into the room, sat at the table, and hurriedly wrote a few lines. Having written her missive, Theresia folded it carefully, and still on tiptoe, more stealthily even than before, she slipped the paper between the young man's loosely clasped fingers. Then, as soundlessly as she had come, she glided out of the room, ran down the passage, and was out in the porch once more, breathless but relieved.

Bertrand had not moved; and no one had seen her. Theresia only paused in the porch long enough to recover her breath, then, without hesitation and with rapid strides, she crossed over to the water's edge and walked along in the direction of the Pent.

Whereupon, the figure of the old cripple emerged from out

the shadows. He gazed after the fast retreating figure of
Theresia for a moment or two, then threw down his load,
straightened out his back, and stretched out his arms from the
shoulders with a sigh of content. After which amazing proceedings he gave a soft, inward chuckle, unstrapped his wooden
leg, slung it with his discarded load across his broad shoulders, and turning his back upon harbour and sea, turned
up the High Street and strode rapidly away.

When Bertrand Moncrif woke, the dawn was peeping in
through the uncurtained window. He felt cold and stiff. He
had been dreaming . . . here in this room . . . Theresia had been
here . . . Then she said that she would come back . . . and he . . .
like a fool . . . had fallen asleep.

He jumped up, fully awake now; and as he did so a folded
scrap of paper fell out of his hand. He had not known that it
was there when first he woke, and somehow it appeared to be
a part of his dream. As it lay there on the sanded floor at his
feet, it looked strangely ghostlike, ominous; and it was with a
trembling hand that, presently, he picked it up.

Every minute now brought fuller daylight into the room; a
grey, cold light, for the window faced the south-west, showing
a wide stretch of the tidal harbour and the open sea beyond.
He went to the window and threw open the casement. Controlling his apprehension, his nervousness, Bertrand at last contrived to unfold the mysterious epistle.

'A kind soul,' so the message ran, 'hath taken compassion on
me. There was no room for me at the inn, and she has offered
me a bed in her cottage, somewhere close by. I do not know
where it is. I have arranged with the landlord that you shall be
left undisturbed. Tomorrow you will go to London with the
de Servals. I will follow later. It is better so. In London you will
find me at the house of Mme. de Neufchateau, a friend of my
father's who lives at No. 54 in Soho Square, and who offered
me hospitality in the days when I thought I might visit London

for pleasure. She will receive me now that I am poor and an exile.'

The letter was signed 'Theresia'.

With that letter in his possession, Bertrand felt that he could not remain indoors. He snatched up his hat and made his way out of the little building.

By the time he reached the harbour, the sun had risen in all its glory. Way out against the translucent sky, the graceful silhouette of the schooner swayed gently in the morning breeze, her outspread sails gleaming like wings that are tinged with gold. Bertrand watched her for awhile. He thought of the mysterious Scarlet Pimpernel and the hideous vengeance which he had wrought against his beloved. With a gesture characteristic of his blood and of his race, he raised his fist and shook it in the direction of the distant ship.

19 | *A meeting*

FOR Marguerite, that wonderful May Day, like so many others equally happy and equally wonderful, came to an end all too soon. To dwell on those winged hours were but to record sorrow, anxiety, a passionate resentment coupled with an equally passionate acceptance of the inevitable.

Then after that came that terrible half-hour, whilst she stood on the landing-stage and watched and watched that tiny speck, the fast-sailing ship that bore her husband away on his errand of mercy and self-sacrifice, leaving her lonely and infinitely desolate.

'Sir Percy not with you tonight, dear Lady Blakeney?'

'With me? Lud love you, no! I have not seen him these three weeks past.'

'The dog!'

When Lady Blakeney was in Richmond, London or Bath, Sir Percy was shooting or fishing or yachting – which was just as it should be. And when he appeared in society, smiling, elegant, always an exquisite, Lady Blakeney would scarce notice him, save for making him a butt for her lively tongue. What it cost Marguerite to keep up this role none but a very few ever knew. The identity of one of the greatest heroes of this or any time was known to his most bitter enemy – not to his friends. His intimates rallied round her, of course: the splendid little band of heroes who formed the League of the Scarlet Pimpernel.

In all these friends then – in their conversation, their happy laughter, their splendid pluck and equally splendid gaiety, the echo of the chief whom they adored – Marguerite found just the solace that she needed. With Lady Ffoulkes and Lady Antony Dewhurst she had everything in common. With those members of the League who happened to be in England, she could talk over and in her mind trace the various stages of the perilous adventure on which her beloved and the others were even then engaged.

Of Madame de Fontenay – for as such Marguerite still knew her – she saw but little. Whether the beautiful Theresia had gone to London or no, whether she had succeeded in finding her truant husband, Marguerite did not know and cared less. Sir Percy, true to his word, had not betrayed the actual identity of Theresia Cabarrus to his wife; but in his light manner had dropped a word or two of warning, which had sharpened Marguerite's suspicions and strengthened her determination to avoid Mme. de Fontenay as far as possible.

One evening Marguerite strolled through the grounds of

Richmond Park with a light foot, and anon reached the monumental gates, through which the exquisite peace and leafy solitude of the Park seemed to beckon insistently to her. The gate was on the latch; she slipped through and struck down a woodland path bordered by tangled undergrowth and tall bracken, and thus reached the pond, when suddenly she perceived Mme. de Fontenay.

A minute or two later, Theresia looked up and in her turn perceived Marguerite.

'Milady!' she exclaimed. 'Ah, I see you at last! I have oft wondered why we never met.'

Marguerite took her hands, greeted her as warmly as she could.

Mme. de Fontenay had not much to relate. She had found refuge in the French convent of the Assumption at Twickenham, where the Mother Superior had been an intimate friend of her mother's in the happy olden days. The sisters had told her that Lady Blakeney's beautiful house was quite near. She would have liked to call – but never dared – hoping for a chance meeting which hitherto had never come.

She asked kindly after milord, and seemed to have heard a rumour that he was at Brighton, in attendance on his royal friend. Of her husband, Mme. de Fontenay had as yet found no trace. He must be living under an assumed name, she thought – no doubt in dire poverty – Theresia feared it, but did not know – would give worlds to find out.

Then she asked Lady Blakeney whether she knew aught of the de Servals.

'I was so interested in them,' she said, 'because I had heard something of them while I was in Paris, and seeing that we arrived in England the same day, though under such different circumstances. But we could not journey to London together, as you, milady, so kindly suggested, because I was very ill the next day ... Ah, can you wonder? ... A kind friend in Dover took care of me. But I remember their name, and have oft marvelled if we should ever meet.'

Yes; Marguerite did see the de Servals from time to time. One of the daughters, Régine, was employed all day at a fashionable dressmaker's in Richmond. The younger girl, Joséphine, was a pupil-teacher at a young ladies' finishing school, and the boy, Jacques, was doing work in a notary's office.

Madame de Fontenay was vastly interested. She hoped that Régine's marriage with the man of her choice would bring a ray of real happiness into the household.

'I hope so too,' Lady Blakeney assented.

'Milady has seen the young man – Régine's fiancé?'

'Oh, yes! Once or twice. But he is engaged in business all day, it seems.'

Whereupon Madame de Fontenay sighed again, and expressed the hope that one day Fate would bring her together with the de Servals.

'We have so much sorrow in common,' she said with a pathetic smile. 'So many misfortunes. We ought to be friends.'

Then she gave a little shiver.

'The weather is extraordinarily cold for July,' she said. 'Ah, how one misses the glorious sunshine of France!'

After which she took her leave, with a gracious inclination of the head and a cordial au revoir. Then she turned off into a small path under the trees, cut through the growing bracken; and Marguerite watched the graceful figure thoughtfully, until the leafy undergrowth hid her from view.

20 | *Departure*

THE next morning's sun rose more radiant than before.

Soon after breakfast Marguerite ordered her coach, intending to go to London in order to visit Lady Ffoulkes and give Sir Andrew the message which was contained for him in Percy's last letter.

Then suddenly she became aware of hurrying footsteps on the gravelled path close by. She turned, and saw a young man whom at first she did not recognize, running with breathless haste towards her. At sight of her he gave a queer cry of excitement and relief.

'Lady Blakeney! Thank God! Thank God!'

Then she recognized him. It was Bertrand Moncrif.

He fell on his knees and seized her gown. He appeared entirely overwrought, unbalanced, and Marguerite tried in vain at first to get a coherent word out of him. All that he kept on repeating was:

'Will you help me? Will you help us all?'

'Indeed I will, if I can, M. Moncrif,' Marguerite said gently. 'Do try and compose yourself and tell me what is amiss.'

She persuaded him to rise, and presently to follow her to a garden seat, where she sat down. He was obviously making an effort to compose himself, and after a little while, he began more coherently:

'Your servants said, milady,' he began, 'that you were in the garden. I could not wait until they called you; so I ran to find you. Will you try and forgive me? I ought not to have intruded.'

'Of course I will forgive you,' Marguerite rejoined with a smile, 'if you will only tell me what is amiss.'

'Régine has gone.'

Marguerite frowned, puzzled, and murmured slowly, not understanding:

'Gone? Whither?'

'To Dover,' he replied, 'with Jacques.'

'Jacques?' she reiterated, still uncomprehending.

'Her brother,' he rejoined. 'You know the boy?'

Marguerite nodded.

'Hot-headed, impulsive,' Moncrif went on, trying to speak calmly. 'He and the girl Joséphine always had it in their minds that they were destined to liberate France from her present state of anarchy and bloodshed.'

'Like you yourself, M. Moncrif!' Marguerite put in with a smile.

'Oh, I became sobered, reasonable, when I realized how futile it all was. We all owe our lives to that noble Scarlet Pimpernel. They were no longer ours to throw away. At least, that was my theory, and Régine's. Jacques of late has been very excited, feverish. And Mme. de Serval has been distraught with anxiety. She worships the boy. But Jacques would not say what was amiss. He spoke to no one. Went to his work every day as usual. Last night he did not come home. A message came for Mme. de Serval to say that a friend in London had persuaded him to go to the play and spend the night with him. Mme. de Serval thought nothing of that. She was pleased to think that Jacques had some amusement to distract him from his brooding thoughts. But Régine, it seems, was not satisfied. After her mother had gone to bed, she went to Jacques's room; found some papers, it seems ... letters ... I know not ... proof in fact that the boy was even then on his way to Dover, having made arrangements to take ship for France.'

'Mon Dieu!' Marguerite exclaimed. 'What senseless folly!'

'Ah! but that is not the worst. Folly, you say. But there is worse folly still.'

He drew a stained and crumpled letter from his pocket.

'She sent me this, this morning,' he said. 'That is why I came to you.'

'You mean Régine?' Marguerite asked, and took the letter which he was handing to her.

'Yes! I did not know what to do ... whom to consult. . . . I have no other friend . . .'

In the meanwhile Marguerite was deciphering the letter.

'My Bertrand,' so the letter ran, 'Jacques is going to France. He says it is his duty. I think that he is mad, and I know that it will kill maman. So I go with him. Perhaps at the last – at Dover – my tears and entreaties might yet prevail. If not, and he puts this senseless project in execution, I can watch over him there, and perhaps save him from too glaring a folly. We go by coach to Dover, which starts in an hour's time. Farewell, my beloved, and forgive me for causing you this anxiety; but I feel that Jacques has more need of me than you.'

Below the signature 'Régine de Serval' there were a few more lines, written as if with an afterthought:

'I have told maman that my employer is sending me down into the country about some dresses for an important customer, and that as Jacques can get a few days' leave from his work, I am taking him with me, for I feel the country air would do him good.

'Maman will be astonished and no doubt hurt that Jacques did not send her a word of farewell, but it is best that she should not learn the truth too suddenly. If we do not return from Dover within the week, you will have to break the news as gently as you can.'

Whilst Marguerite read the letter, Bertrand had sunk upon the seat and buried his head in his hands.

'What was your idea,' she asked, 'in coming to me? What can I do?'

'Give me advice, milady!' he implored. 'I am so helpless, so friendless. When I had the letter, I could think of nothing at first. You see, Régine and Jacques started early this morning, by the coach from London, long before I had it. I thought you could tell me what to do, how to overtake them.'

'You think you can persuade Régine, M. Moncrif?'

'I am sure,' he asserted firmly.

'But there is the boy — Jacques!'

'He is just a child — he acted on impulse — and I always had great authority over him. And you, milady! The whole family worship you! . . . They know what they owe to you.'

Marguerite rose.

'Very well,' she said simply. 'We'll go together and see what we can do with those two obstinate young folk.'

Bertrand gave a gasp of surprise and of hope.

'You, milady?' he murmured. 'You would . . . really . . . help me . . . like that?'

Marguerite smiled.

'I really would help you like that,' she said. 'My coach is ordered; we can start at once. We'll get relays at Maidstone and at Ashford, and easily reach Dover tonight before the arrival of the public coach.'

The coach was actually at the gates. The maids packed the necessary valise; her ladyship changed her smart gown for a dark travelling one, and less than half an hour after Bertrand Moncrif's first arrival at the Manor, he was seated beside Lady Blakeney in her coach. The coachman cracked his whip, the postilion swung himself into the saddle, and the servants stood at attention as the vehicle slowly swung out of the gates, and presently, the horses putting on the pace, disappeared along the road, followed by a cloud of dust.

Bertrand Moncrif, brooding, absorbed in thoughts, said

little or nothing while the coach swung along at a very brisk pace.

Marguerite allowed her thoughts to dwell on these people, whom her husband's splendid sacrifice on their behalf had rendered dear. Indeed, she loved them as she loved so many others, because of the dangers which he had braved for their sakes. Their lives had become valuable because of his precious one, daily risked because of them. And at the back of her mind there was also the certainty that if these two young fools did put their mad project in execution and endeavoured to return to Paris, it would again be the gallant Scarlet Pimpernel who would jeopardize his life to save them from the consequences of their own folly.

Luncheon and a brief halt was taken at Farningham and Maidstone reached by three o'clock in the afternoon. Here Lady Blakeney's own servants took leave of her, and post-horses were engaged to take her ladyship on to Ashford. Two hours later, at Ashford, fresh relays were obtained. The public coach at this hour was only some nine or ten miles ahead, it seems, and there was now every chance that Dover would be reached by nightfall and the young runaways met by their pursuers on arrival.

All was then for the best. Bertrand, after the coach had rattled out of Ashford, began to talk, long and earnestly — of himself, his plans and projects, of Régine herself and the de Servals, mother, son, and daughters. His voice was toneless and very even. The monotony of his diction acted after a while as a soporific on Marguerite's nerves. The rumble of the coach, the closeness of this long afternoon in July, the rocking of the springs, made her feel drowsy. After a while, too, a curious scent pervaded the interior of the coach — a sweet, heady scent that appeared to weigh her eyelids down and gave her a feeling of delicious and lazy beatitude. She laid her head against the cushions, and still she heard the dreary monotone of

Bertrand's voice, quite inarticulate now, like the hum of a swarm of bees . . .

Then, all of a sudden she was full conscious; only just in time to feel the weight of an iron hand against her mouth and to see Bertrand's face, ghastly of hue, eyes distorted more with fear than rage, quite close to her own. The next moment a thick woollen scarf was wound quickly and tightly round her head, covering her mouth and eyes, only barely giving her room to breathe, and her hands and arms were tied together with cords.

This brutal assault had been so quick and sudden that at first it seemed to Marguerite like part of a hideous dream. She was not fully conscious, and was half suffocated by the thick folds of the scarf and that persistent odour, which by its sickening sweetness caused her well-nigh to swoon.

Through this semi-consciousness, however, she was constantly aware of her enemy, Bertrand Moncrif – the black-hearted traitor who had carried out this execrable outrage: why and for what purpose, Marguerite was too dazed to attempt to guess. He was there, that she knew. She was conscious of his hands making sure of the cords round her wrists, tightening the scarf around her mouth; then presently she felt him leaning across her body and throwing down the window, and she heard him shouting to the driver:

'Her ladyship has fainted. Drive as fast as ever you can till you come to that white house yonder on the right, the one with the green shutters and the tall yew at the gate!'

The driver's reply she could not hear, nor the crack of his whip. A few minutes went by – an eternity. Then that terrible cloying perfume was again held close to her nostrils; an awful dizziness and nausea seized her; after which she remembered nothing more.

21 | *Memories*

WHEN Marguerite Blakeney recovered consciousness, the sun was low down in the west. She was in a coach – not her own – which was being whisked along the road at terrific speed. She was alone, her mouth gagged, her wrists and her ankles tied with cords, so that she could neither speak nor move – a helpless log, being taken . . . whither? . . . and by whom?

Through the front window of the coach she could perceive the vague outline of two men sitting on the driver's seat, whilst another was riding the off-leader. Marguerite had seen too much of the cruelties and barbarities of this world, too much of the hatred that existed between enemy countries, and too much of the bitter rancour felt by certain men against her husband and indirectly against herself, not to realize at once whence the blow had come that had struck her. This was the work of her husband's enemies, who, through her, were once more striving to get at him.

The embarkation took place somewhere on the coast around Birchington. She was lifted out of the coach, and at once a shawl was thrown over her face, so that she could not see. Birchington seemed the natural objective of the miscreants who had her in their power. In fact, at one moment she was quite sure that the square tower of old Minster church flitted past her vision through the window of the coach, and that the horses immediately after that sprinted the hill between Minster and Acoll.

For a while she lay at the bottom of a small boat, aching in body as well as in mind, her eyes closed, her limbs cramped by the cords which owing to the damp were cutting into her flesh, faint with cold and want of food, wet to the skin yet with eyes and head and hands burning hot, and her ears filled with the dreary, monotonous sound of the oars creaking in the rowlocks and the boom of the water against the sides of the boat.

She was lifted out of the boat and carried, as she judged, by two men up a companion ladder, then down some steps and finally deposited on some hard boards; after which the wet shawl was removed from her face. She was in the dark. Only a tiny streak of light found its way through a chink somewhere close to the floor. A smell of tar and of stale food gave her a wretched sense of nausea. After a while the familiar motion, the well-known sound of a ship weighing anchor, gave another blow to her few lingering hopes.

She was taken ashore in the early dawn, at a spot not very far from Boulogne. Precautions were no longer taken against her possible calls for help; even the cords had been removed from her wrists and ankles as soon as she was lowered into the boat that brought her to shore.

All the faces around her were unfamiliar. There were four or five men, surly and silent, who piloted her over the rocks and cliffs and then along the sands, to the little hamlet of Wimereux, which she knew well.

Later on, in a squalid little hovel on the outskirts of Wimereux, she was at last given some food which, though of the poorest and roughest description, was nevertheless welcome, for it revived her spirit and strengthened her courage, of which she had sore need.

The rest of the journey was uneventful. Within the first hour of making a fresh start, she had realized that she was being taken to Paris.

Paris was reached at dawn of the third day. Seventy-two hours had crept along, leaden-footed, since the moment when she had stepped into her own coach outside her beautiful home in Richmond, surrounded by her own servants, and with that traitor Moncrif by her side. Since then, what a load of sorrow, of anxiety, of physical and mental suffering had she borne! And yet, even that sorrow, even those sufferings and that anxiety, seemed as nothing beside the heart-rending thoughts of her beloved, as yet ignorant of her terrible fate and of the schemes which those who had so shamefully trapped her were even now concocting for the realization of their vengeance against him.

22 | *Waiting*

THE house to which Marguerite was ultimately driven, and where she presently found herself ushered up the stairs into a small, well-furnished apartment, appeared to be situated somewhere in an outlying quarter of Paris.

The apartment consisted of three rooms – a bedroom, a sitting-room, and small cabinet de toilette – all plainly but nicely furnished. An old woman, dour of mien but otherwise willing and attentive, did all she could to minister to the poor wearied woman's wants. She brought up some warm milk and home-baked bread. Butter, she explained, was not obtainable these days, and the household had not seen sugar for weeks.

Marguerite, tired out and hungry, readily ate some breakfast; but what she longed for most and needed most was rest. So presently, at the gruff invitation of the old woman, she undressed and stretched her weary limbs between the sheets.

When she woke, it was late afternoon. On a chair close by her bedside was some clean linen laid out, a change of stockings, clean shoes, and a gown. Marguerite rose and dressed. The linen was fine, obviously the property of a woman of refinement. A while later, the dour attendant brought her some soup and a dish of cooked vegetables.

With the sense of well-being further accentuated by the feel of warm, dry clothes and of wholesome food, Marguerite had her mind free enough to think and to ponder. She had thrown open the window, and found that she was gazing out in the direction of the north-west, that the apartment wherein she found herself was on the top floor of a detached house which, judging by certain landmarks vaguely familiar, was situated somewhere outside the barrier of St. Antoine, and not very far from the Bastille and from the Arsenal.

Where was she? Why was she being treated with a kindness and consideration altogether at variance with the tactics usually adopted by the enemies of the Scarlet Pimpernel? She was not in prison. She was not being starved, or threatened, or humiliated.

But though Marguerite Blakeney was not in prison, she was a prisoner. This she had ascertained five minutes after she was alone in the apartment. She could wander at will from room to room; but only in them, not out of them. The door of communication between the rooms was wide open; those that obviously gave on a landing outside were securely locked; and when a while ago the old woman had entered with the tray of food, Marguerite had caught sight of a group of men in the well-known tattered uniform of the National Guard, standing at attention in a wide, long antechamber.

Thus for twenty-four hours was she left to meditate, thrown upon her own resources, with no other company save that of her own thoughts, and they were anything but cheerful. The uncertainty of the situation soon began to prey upon her nerves.

She had been calm in the morning; but as the day wore on the loneliness, the mystery, the silence, began to tell upon her courage. Soon she got to look upon the woman who waited on her as her jailer, and when she was alone she was for ever straining her ears to hear what the men who were guarding her door might be saying among themselves.

The next night she hardly slept.

Twenty-four hours later she had a visit from citizen Chauvelin. He began by asking solicitously after her well-being; hoped the journey had not over-fatigued her; humbly begged her pardon for the discomfort which a higher power compelled him to put upon her. Marguerite, exasperated, and her nerves on edge, curtly bade him to come to the point.

'I have come to the point, dear lady,' he retorted suavely. 'This point is that you should be comfortable and have no cause to complain whilst you are under this roof.'

'And how long am I to remain a prisoner under it?' she asked.

'Until Sir Percy has in his turn honoured this house with his presence,' he replied.

He waited for her to speak, his pale eyes, slightly mocking, fixed upon her. Then she said simply:

'I understand.'

'I was quite sure you would, dear lady,' he rejoined blandly. 'You see, the phase of heroics is past. The beautiful Lady Blakeney is a guest under this roof. Well, sooner or later that most gallant of husbands will desire to approach his lady. Sooner or later he will learn that she is no longer in England. Then he will set his incomparable wits to work to find out where she is. Again, I may say that sooner or later, perhaps, even aided by us, he will know that she is here. Then he will come. Am I not right?'

Of course he was right. Sooner or later Percy would learn

where she was; and then he would come. Now there was no alternative, no deep-laid plot save one: to wait for the Scarlet Pimpernel until he came.

23 | *Mice and men*

IT was on her return from England that Theresia Cabarrus took to consulting the old witch in the Rue de la Planchette, driven thereto by ambition, and also no doubt by remorse. The Scarlet Pimpernel had appeared before her as one utterly impervious to her charms, and, egged on by Chauvelin, who used her for his own ends, she entered into a callous conspiracy, the aim of which was the destruction of that gang of English spies who were the enemies of France, and the first stage of which was the heartless abduction of Lady Blakeney and her incarceration as a decoy for the ultimate capture of her own husband.

Thus Theresia had attained one of her great desires: the Scarlet Pimpernel was as good as captured, and when he finally succumbed he could not fail to know whence came the blow that struck him.

Something of the glamour which had originally surrounded Mother Théot's incantations had vanished since sixty-two of her devotees had been sent to the guillotine on a charge of conspiring for the overthrow of the Republic.

To those, however, who chose to defy public opinion and to disregard the dangers which attended the frequentation of Mother Théot's sorceries, these latter had lost little or nothing of their pristine solemnity. There was the closely curtained room; the scented, heavy atmosphere; the chants, the coloured flames.

Theresia, sitting on the dais, was drinking in the honeyed words and flattering prophecies of the old witch.

'Thy name will be the greatest in the land! At thy word heads will fall and diadems will totter!' Mother Théot announced in sepulchral tones, whilst gazing into the crystal before her.

'As the wife of citizen Tallien?' Theresia queried in an awed whisper.

'That the spirits do not say,' the old witch replied. 'What is a name to them? I see a crown of glory, and thy head surrounded by a golden light; and at thy feet lies something which once was scarlet, and now is crimson and crushed.'

'What does it mean?' Theresia murmured.

'That is for thee to know,' the sybil replied sternly. 'Commune with the spirits; lose thyself in their embrace; learn from them the great truths, and the future will be made clear to thee.'

With which cryptic utterance she gathered her veils around her and glided out of the room.

But directly she had closed the door behind her, Mother Théot's manner underwent a change. She became just an ugly old woman, wrinkled and hook-nosed, dressed in shabby draperies that were grey with age and dirt, and with claw-like hands that looked like the talons of a bird of prey.

As she entered the room, a man who had been standing at the window opposite, staring into the dismal street below, turned quickly to her.

'Art satisfied?' she asked at once.

'From what I could hear, yes!' he replied, 'though I could have wished thy pronouncements had been more clear.'

The hag shrugged her lean shoulders and nodded in the direction of her lair.

'Oh!' she said. 'The Spaniard understands well enough. She never consults me or invokes the spirits but they speak to her of that which is scarlet. She knows what it means. You need not fear, citizen Chauvelin, that in the pursuit of her vaulting ambition, she will forget that her primary duty is to you!'

'No,' Chauvelin asserted calmly, 'she'll not forget that. The Cabarrus is no fool. She knows well enough that when citizens of the State have been employed to work on its behalf, they are no longer free agents afterwards. The work must be carried through to the end.'

'You need not fear the Cabarrus, citizen,' the sybil rejoined dryly. 'She'll not fail you. Her vanity is immense. She believes that the Englishman insulted her by writing that flippant letter, and she'll not leave him alone till she has had her revenge.'

'No!' Chauvelin assented. 'She'll not fail me. Nor thou either, citoyenne.'

The old hag shrugged her shoulders.

'I?' she exclaimed, with a quiet laugh. 'Is that likely? You promised me ten thousand livres the day the Scarlet Pimpernel is captured!'

'And the guillotine,' Chauvelin broke in grimly, 'if thou shouldst allow the woman upstairs to escape.'

'I know that,' the old woman rejoined dryly. 'If she escapes 'twill not be through my connivance. Have no fear, citizen Chauvelin.'

'That's brave! And now, tell me what has become of the coal-heaver Rateau?'

'Oh, he comes and goes. You told me to encourage him. So I gave him potions for his cough. He has one foot in the grave.'

'Would he had both!' Chauvelin broke in savagely. 'That man is a perpetual menace to my plans. It would have been so much better if we could have sent him last April to the guillotine.'

'It was in your hands,' Mother Théot retorted. 'The Committee reported against him. Aiding that execrable Scarlet Pimpernel to escape . . .! Name of a name! it should have been enough!'

'It was not proved that he did aid the English spies,' Chauvelin retorted moodily. 'And Foucquier-Tinville would not arraign him. Tell me more about Rateau. Does he often come here?'

'Yes; very often. He must be in my anteroom now. He came directly he was let out of prison, and has haunted this place ever since. He thinks I can cure him of his asthma, and as he pays me well –'

'Pays you well?' Chauvelin broke in quickly.

'Rateau is no starveling,' the old woman asserted. 'Many an English gold piece hath he given me.'

'But not of late?'

'Not later than yesterday.'

'Then he is still in touch with that cursed Englishman.'

Mother Théot shrugged her shoulders.

'Does one ever know which is the Englishman and which the asthmatic Rateau?' she queried, with a dry laugh.

Whereupon a strange thing happened – so strange indeed that Chauvelin's next words turned to savage curses, and that Mother Théot, white to the lips, her knees shaking under her, tiny beads of perspiration rising beneath her scanty locks, had to hold on to the table to save herself from falling.

And yet nothing very alarming had occurred. Only a man had laughed, light-heartedly and long; and the sound of that laughter had come from somewhere near – the next room probably, or the landing beyond Mother Théot's anteroom.

A man had laughed. One of Mother Théot's clients probably, who in the company of a friend chose to while away the weary hour of waiting on the sybil by hilarious conversation. Of course, that was it! Chauvelin, cursing himself now for his cowardice, passed a still shaking hand across his brow.

'One of your clients is of good cheer,' he said with well-assumed indifference.

'There is no one in the anteroom at this hour,' the old hag murmured under her breath. 'Only Rateau ... and he is too scant of breath to laugh ... he ...'

But Chauvelin no longer heard what she had to say. With an exclamation which no one who heard it could have defined, he turned on his heel and almost ran out of the room.

24 | *By order of the State*

THE antechamber was empty. Mother Théot, voluble and quaking with fear, was close at his heels.

'I was dreaming, of course,' he muttered aloud to himself between his teeth. 'I have that arch-devil, his laugh, his voice, his affectations, on the brain!'

He was on the point of going to the main door, in order to peer out on the landing or down the stairs, when he heard his name called immediately behind him. Theresia Cabarrus was standing under the lintel of the door which gave on the sybil's sanctum, her delicate hand holding back the *portière*.

'Citizen Chauvelin,' she said, 'I was waiting for you.'

'And I, citoyenne,' he retorted gruffly, 'had in truth forgotten you.'

'Mother Théot left me alone for a while, to commune with the spirits,' she explained.

'Ah!' he riposted, slightly sarcastic. 'With what result?'

'To help you further, citizen Chauvelin,' she replied; 'if you have need of me.'

'Ah!' he exclaimed with a savage curse. 'In truth, I have need of every willing hand that will raise itself against mine enemy. I have need of you, citizeness; of every patriot who will sit and watch this house, to which we have brought the one bait that will lure the goldfish to our net.'

'Have I not proved my willingness, citizen?' she retorted, with a smile. 'Think you 'tis pleasant to give up my life, my salon, my easy, contented existence, and become a mere drudge in your service?'

'A drudge,' he broke in with a chuckle, 'who will soon be greater than a Queen.'

'Ah, if I thought that! . . .' she exclaimed.

'I am as sure of it as that I am alive,' he replied firmly. 'You will never do anything with citizen Tallien, citoyenne. He is too mean, too cowardly. But bring the Scarlet Pimpernel to his knees at the chariot wheel of Robespierre, and even the crown of the Bourbons would be yours for the asking!'

'I know that, citizen,' she rejoined dryly; 'else I were not here.'

'We hold all the winning cards,' he went on eagerly, 'Lady Blakeney is in our hands. So long as we hold her, we have the certainty that sooner or later the English spy will establish communication with her. Catherine Théot is a good jailer, and Captain Byer upstairs has a number of men under his command whose efficiency I can guarantee and whose eagerness is stimulated by the promise of a magnificent reward. But experience has taught me that the accursed Scarlet Pimpernel is never so dangerous as when we think we hold him. That is why, citoyenne, I dragged you to England; that is why I placed you face to face with him, and said to you, "That is the man." Since then, with your help, we hold the decoy. In your eyes I place my trust; in your wits, your instinct. In whatever guise the

Scarlet Pimpernel presents himself before you – and he *will* present himself before you, or he is no longer the impudent and reckless adventurer I know him to be! – I feel that you at least will recognize him.'

'Yes; I think I should recognize him,' she mused.

'Bring the Scarlet Pimpernel to his knees, citoyenne, and Robespierre will be as much your slave as he is now the prey to a strange dread of that one man. Robespierre fears the Scarlet Pimpernel. Ah, citoyenne! what influence you would have over him if through your agency all those fears could be drowned in the blood of that abominable Englishman!'

'Now, who would have thought that?' a mocking voice broke in suddenly, with a quiet chuckle. 'I vow, my dear M. Chambertin, you are waxing more eloquent than ever before!'

Like the laughter of a while ago, the voice seemed to come from nowhere. It was in the air, muffled by the clouds of Mother Théot's perfumes, or by the thickness of doors and tapestries.

'By Satan, this is intolerable!' Chauvelin exclaimed; and paying no heed to Theresia's faint cry of terror, he ran to the main door. It was on the latch. He tore it open and dashed out upon the landing.

The staircase received its only light from a small window high up in the roof, the panes of which were coated with grime, so that the well of the stairs, especially past the first-floor landing, was almost in complete gloom.

Chauvelin ran down half a dozen steps, peered down the shaft of the staircase and spied a tiny light, which moved swiftly to and fro. Then the light disappeared. For a second or two the darkness appeared more impenetrably dense; then one or two narrow streaks of daylight showed the position of the outside door. Something prompted him to call:

'Is that you, citizen Rateau?'

It was foolish, of course. And the very next moment he had

his answer. A voice – the mocking voice he knew so well – called up to him in reply:

'At your service, dear M. Chambertin! Can I do anything for you?'

Chauvelin threw all prudence to the winds, and ran down the stairs as fast as his shaking knees would allow him. Some three steps from the bottom he paused. The figure in the gloom looked very large, and the flickering light threw fantastic shadows on the face and neck of the colossus, distorting the nose to a grotesque length and the chin to weird proportions.

The next instant Chauvelin gave a cry like an enraged bull and hurled his meagre person upon the giant, who, shaken at the moment by a tearing fit of coughing, was taken unawares and fell backwards, overborne by the impact, dropping the light as he fell and still wheezing pitiably.

Chauvelin, vaguely surprised at his own strength or the weakness of his opponent, pressed his knee against the latter's chest and gripped him by the throat.

'At my service, in truth, my gallant Pimpernel!' he murmured hoarsely. 'What you can do for me? Wait here, until I have you bound and gagged, safe against further mischief!'

His victim had in fact given a last convulsive gasp, lay now at full length upon the stone floor, with arms outstretched, motionless. Chauvelin relaxed his grip. His strength was spent, he was bathed in sweat, his body shook from head to foot. But he was triumphant! His mocking enemy, carried away by his own histrionics, had overtaxed his colossal strength. The carefully simulated fit of coughing had taken away his breath at the critical moment; the surprise attack had done the rest; and Chauvelin had conquered by sheer pluck and resource.

There lay the Scarlet Pimpernel, who had assumed the guise of asthmatic Rateau once too often, helpless and broken beneath the weight of the man whom he had hoodwinked and derided. And now at last all the intrigues, the humiliations, the schemes, and the disappointments, were at an end. He – Chauvelin – free and honoured: Robespierre his grateful servant.

A wave of dizziness passed over his brain – the dizziness of coming glory. When he staggered to his feet he could scarcely stand. He lurched up to the door, fumbled for the latch of the wicket-gate, and finding it pulled the gate open and almost fell out into the open.

He called for help with all his might.

Within two or three minutes, half a dozen men of the National Guard were speeding down the street. Soon they had reached the house, the door where Chauvelin gave them hasty instructions.

'The man lying on the ground in there,' he commanded. 'Seize him and raise him. Then one of you find some cord and bind him securely.'

The men flung the double doors wide open. There lay the huge figure on the floor, no longer motionless, but trying to scramble to his feet, once more torn by a fit of coughing. The men ran up to him; one of them laughed.

'Why, if it isn't old Rateau!'

They lifted him up by his arms. He was helpless as a child, and his face was of a dull purple colour.

'He will die!' another man said, with an indifferent shrug of the shoulders.

They had succeeded in propping him up and sitting him down upon a barrel. He raised his head and encountered the pale eyes of citizen Chauvelin fixed as if sightlessly upon him.

'Name of a dog!' he began; but got no further. Giddiness seized him, for he was weak from coughing and from that strangling grip round his throat, after he had been attacked in the darkness and thrown violently to the ground.

The men around him recoiled at sight of citizen Chauvelin. His appearance was almost death-like. His cheeks and lips were livid; his hair dishevelled; his eyes of an unearthly paleness.

He gazed on Rateau for a moment or two, his eyes travelling over the uncouth, semi-conscious figure of the coalheaver with a searching glance. Then, as if suddenly struck with an idea, he spoke to the man nearest him:

'Sergeant Chazot? Is he at the Arsenal?'

'Yes, citizen,' the man replied.

'Run across quickly then,' Chauvelin continued; 'and bring him thither at once.'

The soldier obeyed, and a few more minutes – ten, perhaps – went by in silence. Rateau, weary, cursing, not altogether in full possession of his faculties, sat huddled upon the barrel, his bleary eyes following every movement of citizen Chauvelin with an anxious, furtive gaze.

The soldier returned, was even now in the doorway with a comrade – a short, thick-set, powerful-looking fellow – beside him.

'Sergeant Chazot!' Chauvelin said abruptly.

'At your commands, citizen!' the sergeant replied, and at a sign from the other followed him to the most distant corner of the room.

'Bend your ear and listen,' Chauvelin murmured peremptorily. 'I don't want those fools to hear.' He pointed to Rateau, then went on rapidly: 'You will take this lout over to the cavalry barracks. See the veterinary. The veterinary, you understand? He brands the horses for the cavalry. I want a brand on this lout's arm. Just a letter . . . a distinguishing mark . . .'

Chazot gave an involuntary gasp.

'But, citizen –!' he exclaimed.

'Eh? What?' the other retorted sharply. 'In the service of the Republic there is no "but", Sergeant Chazot.'

'I know that, citizen,' Chazot, abashed, murmured humbly. 'I only meant . . . it seems so strange . . .'

'Stranger things than that occur every day in Paris, my friend,' Chauvelin said dryly. 'We brand horses that are the property of the State; why not a man?'

' 'Tis not for me to argue, citizen,' Chazot rejoined. 'If you tell me to take citizen Rateau over to the veterinary at the cavalry barracks and have him branded like cattle, why . . .'

'Not like cattle, citizen,' Chauvelin broke in blandly. 'You shall commence proceedings by administering to citizen Rateau a whole bottle of excellent eau de vie, at the Government's expense. Then, when he is thoroughly and irretrievably drunk, the veterinary will put the brand upon his left forearm . . . just one letter . . . Why, the drunken reprobate will never feel it!'

'As you command, citizen,' Chazot assented with perfect indifference. 'I am not responsible. I do as I'm told.'

'Like the fine soldier that you are, citizen Chazot!' Chauvelin concluded.

He took tablet and point from his pocket and scribbled a few words.

Chazot took the written order and slipped it into his pocket. Then he briefly gave the necessary orders to the men. Once more they hoisted the helpless giant up on his feet.

Chauvelin watched the little party file out of the place, then cross the Rue le da Planchette and take the turning opposite the one that led through the Porte and the Rue St. Antoine to the cavalry barracks in the Quartier Bastille. After which, he carefully closed the double outside doors and groped his way to the foot of the stairs and slowly mounted to the floor above.

He reached the first-floor landing. The door which led into Mother Théot's apartments was on the latch, and Chauvelin had just stretched out his hand with a view to pushing it open, when the door swung out on its hinges, as if moved by an invisible hand, and a pleasant, mocking voice immediately behind him said, with grave politeness:

'Allow me, my dear M. Chambertin!'

25 | *Four days*

WHAT occurred during the next few seconds Chauvelin himself would have been least able to say. Certain it is that, when he returned to the full realization of things, he was sitting on one of the benches, his back against the wall, whilst immediately in front of him, looking down on him through half-closed, lazy eyes, debonair, well groomed, unperturbed, stood his arch-enemy, Sir Percy Blakeney.

Of Theresia Cabarrus there was not a sign.

'You are looking for Mme. de Fontenay, I believe, dear M. Chambertin,' Sir Percy said lightly, as if divining his thoughts. 'The ladies – ah, the ladies! Alas!' he went on with mock affection, 'that Mme. de Fontenay should have fled at first sound of my voice! Now she hath sought refuge in the old witch's lair, there to consult the spirits as to how best she can get out again, seeing that the door is now locked ... Demmed awkward, a locked door, when a pretty woman wants to be on the other side. What think you, M. Chambertin?'

'I only think, Sir Percy,' Chauvelin contrived to retort, calling all his wits and all his courage to aid him in his humiliating position, 'I only think of another pretty woman, who is in the room just above our heads, and who would also be mightily glad to find herself the other side of a locked door.'

'Your thoughts,' Sir Percy retorted with a light laugh, 'are always so ingenuous, my dear M. Chambertin. Strangely enough, mine just at this moment run on the possibility – not a very unlikely one, you will admit – of shaking the breath out of your ugly little body.'

'Shake, my dear Sir Percy, shake,' Chauvelin replied with well-simulated calm. 'I grant you that I am a puny rat and you the most magnificent of lions; but even if I lie mangled and breathless on this stone floor at your feet, Lady Blakeney will still be a prisoner in our hands. I only desire to explain to you, Sir Percy, the dangers to which you expose Lady Blakeney, if you laid violent hands upon me. 'Tis you, remember, who sought this interview – not I.'

'You are right, my dear sir, always right. I pray you to proceed.'

'Allow me then to make my point clear. There are at this moment a score of men of the National Guard in the room above your head. Every one of them goes to the guillotine if they allow their prisoner to escape; every one of them receives a reward of ten thousand livres the day they capture the Scarlet Pimpernel. But that is not all,' Chauvelin went on quite steadily, seeing that Sir Percy had apparently become thoughtful and absorbed. 'The men are under the command of Captain Boyer, and he understands that every day at a certain hour – seven in the evening, to be precise – I will be with him and interrogate him as to the welfare of the prisoner. If – mark me, Sir Percy! – if on any one day I do not appear before him at that hour, his orders are to shoot the prisoner on sight . . .'

The word was scarce out of his mouth; it broke in a hoarse spasm. Sir Percy had him by the throat.

'You cur!' he said in an ominous whisper, his face quite close now to that of his enemy, his jaw set, his eyes no longer good-humoured and mildly scornful, but burning with the fire of a mighty, unbridled wrath.

Then suddenly his grip relaxed, the whole face changed as if an unseen hand had swept away the fierce lines of anger and of hate. The eyes softened beneath their heavy lids, the set lips broke into a mocking smile. He let go his hold of the Terrorist's throat; and the unfortunate man, panting and breathless, fell heavily against the wall. He tried to steady himself as best he could, but his knees were shaking, and faint and helpless, he finally collapsed upon the nearest bench, the while Sir Percy straightened out his tall figure, with unruffled composure rubbed his slender hands one against the other, as if to free them from dust, and said, with gentle, good-humoured sarcasm:

'Do put your cravat straight, man! You look a disgusting object!'

He dragged the corner of a bench forward, sat astride upon it, and waited with perfect sang-froid, spy-glass in hand, while Chauvelin mechanically readjusted the set of his clothes.

'That's better,' he said approvingly. 'Just the bow at the back of your neck . . . a little more to the right . . . now your cuffs . . . Ah, you look quite tidy again!'

'Sir Percy –!' Chauvelin broke in with a vicious snarl.

'I entreat you to accept my apologies,' the other rejoined with utmost courtesy. 'I was on the verge of losing my temper, which we in England would called demmed bad form. I'll not transgress again. I pray you, proceed with what you were saying. So interesting – demmed interesting! You were talking, about murdering a woman in cold blood, I think –'

'In hot blood, Sir Percy,' Chauvelin rejoined more firmly. 'Blood fired by thoughts of a just revenge. Had you ceased to interfere in the affairs of France, you would not now be in the sorry plight in which your own intrigues have at last landed you. Had you left us alone, we should by now have forgotten you.'

'Which would have been such a pity, my dear M. Chambertin,' Blakeney rejoined gravely. 'I should not like you to forget me. Believe me, I have enjoyed life so much these past two years, I would not give up those pleasures even for that of seeing you and your friends have a bath or wear tidy buckles on your shoes.'

'You will have cause to indulge in those pleasures within the next few days, Sir Percy,' Chauvelin rejoined dryly.

'What?' Sir Percy exclaimed. 'The Committee of Public Safety going to have a bath? Or the Revolutionary Tribunal? Which?'

But Chauvelin was determined not to lose his temper again.

'The pleasure of pitting your wits against the inevitable,' he riposted dryly.

'Ah? You really mean this time – ?' and Sir Percy made a significant gesture across his own neck.

'In as few days as possible.'

Whereupon Sir Percy rose, and said solemnly:

'You are right there, my friend, quite right. Delays are always dangerous. If you mean to have my head, why – have it quickly. As for me, delays always bore me to tears.'

He yawned and stretched his long limbs.

'I am getting so demmed fatigued,' he said. 'Do you not think this conversation has lasted quite long enough!'

'It was none of my seeking, Sir Percy.'

'Mine, I grant you; mine, absolutely! But, hang it, man! I had to tell you that your breeches were badly cut.'

'We await your pleasure, Sir Percy. Lady Blakeney must not be kept in suspense too long. Shall we say that, in three days . . . ?'

'Make it four, my dear M. Chambertin, and I am eternally your debtor.'

'In four days then, Sir Percy,' Chauvelin rejoined with pronounced sarcasm. 'You see how ready I am to meet you in a spirit of conciliation! Four days, you say? Very well then; for

four days more we keep our prisoner in those rooms upstairs
. . . After that . . . After that, Captain Boyer has orders to shoot
her.'

Just one second, whilst Chauvelin waited for his enemy's
answer to this monstrous pronouncement, and the very walls
of the drab apartment appeared to listen, expectant.

'You really are the worst-dressed man I have ever come
across, my good M. Chambertin,' Sir Percy said with rare good-
humour. 'No decent man would be seen walking up the guillotine in such a waistcoat as you are wearing. As for your boots –'
He yawned again. 'You really must excuse me! I came late
from the theatre last night, and have not had my usual hours
of sleep. So, by your leave –'

'By all means, Sir Percy!' Chauvelin replied complacently.
'At this moment you are a free man, because I happen to be
alone and unarmed, and because this house is solidly built and
my voice would not carry to the floor above. Also because you
are so nimble that no doubt you could give me the slip long
before Captain Boyer and his men came to my rescue. Yes, Sir
Percy; for the moment you are a free man! Free to walk out
of this house unharmed. But even now, you are not as free as
you would wish to be, eh?'

Whereupon Blakeney threw up his head and laughed
heartily.

'You are absolutely priceless, my dear M. Chambertin!' he
said gaily. 'But you really must put your cravat straight. It has
once again become disarranged . . . in the heat of your oratory,
no doubt . . . Allow me to offer you a pin.'

And with inimitable affection, he took a pin out of his
own cravat and presented it to Chauvelin.

'Your insults leave me unmoved, Sir Percy,' Chauvelin broke
in savagely, and tried to free himself from the touch of those
slender, strong hands that wandered so uncomfortably in the
vicinity of his throat.

'No doubt,' Blakeney riposted lightly, 'that they are as futile as your threats. One does not insult a cur, any more than one threatens Sir Percy Blakeney – what?'

'You are right, Sir Percy. The time for threats has gone by. And since you appear so vastly entertained –'

'I *am* vastly entertained, my dear M. Chambertin! How can I help it, when I see before me a miserable shred of humanity who does not even know how to keep his tie straight or his hair smooth, calmly – or almost calmly – talking of – Let me see, what were you talking of, my amiable friend?'

'Of the hostage, Sir Percy, which we hold until the happy day when the gallant Scarlet Pimpernel is a prisoner in our hands.'

' 'M, yes! He was that once before, was he not, my good sir? Then, too, you laid down mighty schemes for his capture.'

'And we succeeded.'

'By your usual amiable methods – lies, deceit, forgery. The latter has been useful to you this time too, eh?'

'What do you mean, Sir Percy?'

'You had need of the assistance of a fair lady for your schemes. She appeared disinclined to help you. So when her inconvenient lover, Bertrand Moncrif, was happily dragged away from her path, you forged a letter, which the lady rightly looked upon as an insult. Because of that letter, she nourished a comfortable amount of spite against me, and lent you her aid in the fiendish outrage for which you are about to receive punishment.'

He had raised his voice slightly while he spoke, and Chauvelin cast an apprehensive glance in the direction of the door behind which he guessed that Theresia Cabarrus must be straining her ears to listen.

'A pretty story, Sir Percy,' he said with affected coolness

'And one that does infinite credit to your imagination. It is mere surmise on your part.'

'What, my friend? What is surmise? That you gave a letter to Madame de Fontenay which you had concocted, and which I had never written? Why, man,' he added with a laugh, 'I saw you do it!'

'You? Impossible!'

'More impossible things than that will happen within the next few days, my good sir. I was outside the window of Madame de Fontenay's apartment during the whole of your interview with her. But why argue about it, my dear M. Chambertin, when you know quite well that I have given you a perfectly accurate exposé of the means which you employed to make a pretty and spoilt woman help you in your nefarious work?'

'Why argue indeed?' Chauvelin retorted dryly. 'Your concern and mine, my gallant friend, is solely with the future – with the next four days, in fact . . . After which, either the Scarlet Pimpernel is in our hands, or Lady Blakeney will be put against the wall upstairs and summarily shot.'

Then only did something of his habitual lazy nonchalance go out of Blakeney's attitude. Just for the space of a few seconds he drew himself up to his full magnificent height, and from the summit of his splendid audacity and the consciousness of his own power, he looked down at the mean, cringing figure of the enemy who had hurled this threat of death against the woman he worshipped.

'And you really believe,' Sir Percy Blakeney said slowly and deliberately, 'that you have the power to carry through your infamous schemes? That I – yes, I! – would allow you to come within measurable distance of your execution? Bah! my dear friend. You have learned nothing by past experience – not even this: that when you dared to lay your filthy hands upon Lady Blakeney, you and the whole pack of assassins who have terrorized this beautiful country far too long, struck the knell of your ultimate doom. You have dared to measure your strength against mine by perpetrating an outrage so monstrous in my sight that, to punish you, I – even I! – will sweep you off the face of the earth and send you to join the pack of unclean ghouls who have aided you in your crimes.'

Chauvelin made a vain effort to laugh, to shrug his shoulders, to put on those airs of insolence which came so naturally to his opponent. No doubt the strain of this long interview with his enemy had told upon his nerves. He closed his eyes, for he felt giddy and sick. When he opened his eyes again he was alone.

26 | *A dream*

CHAUVELIN had not yet regained full possession of his faculties, when a few seconds later he saw Theresia Cabarrus glide swiftly across the antechamber.

Outside on the landing she paused. She ran down a few steps, then called softly:

'Milord!'

A pleasant voice gave quiet reply:

'At your service, fair lady!'

Theresia, shrewd as well as brave, continued to descend.

Midway down the stairs she came face to face with him, and when she paused, panting, a little breathless with excitement, he said with perfect courtesy:

'You did me the honour to call me, Madame?'

'Yes, milord,' she replied, in a quick, eager whisper. 'I heard every word that passed between you and citizen Chauvelin. That letter, milord –'

'Which letter, Madame?'

'That insulting letter to me . . . when you took Moncrif away . . . You never wrote it?'

'Did you really think that I did?' he retorted.

'No. I ought to have guessed . . . the moment that I saw you in England . . .'

'And realized that I was not a cad – what?'

'Milord,' she said abruptly, 'you told me once – you remember? – that you were what you English call a sportsman. Is that so?'

'I hope always to remain that, dear lady,' he replied with a smile.

'Does that mean,' she queried, 'does that mean a man who would under no circumstances harm a woman?'

'I think so.'

'Not even if she – if she has sinned – transgressed against him?'

'I don't quite understand, Madame,' he rejoined simply. 'And, time being short – Are you perchance speaking of yourself?'

'Yes. I have done you an injury, milord,' she replied earnestly. 'I was deceived by that abominable liar, who knew how to play upon a woman's pique. Oh, cannot you believe me? And I would give worlds to atone!'

He laughed in his quiet, gently ironical way.

'You do not happen to possess worlds, dear lady. All that you have is youth and beauty and ambition, and life. You would forfeit all those treasures if you really tried to atone.'

'But –'

'Lady Blakeney is a prisoner . . . You are her jailer . . . Her precious life is the hostage for yours. If you ran counter to your friend Chauvelin's desires, that pretty neck of yours would suffer. A thing to be avoided at all costs! And now,' he added, 'have I your permission to go? My position here is somewhat precarious, and for the next four days I cannot afford the luxury of entertaining so fair a lady, by running my head into a noose.'

'Milord!' she pleaded.

'At your service, dear lady!'

'Is there naught I can do for you?'

'You can ask Lady Blakeney to forgive you,' he said.

'And if she does?'

'She will know what to do, to convey her thoughts to me.'

'Nay! but I'll do more than that, milord,' Theresia continued excitedly. 'I will tell her that I shall pray night and day for your deliverance and hers. I will tell her that I have seen you, and that you are well.'

'Ah, if you did that –!' he exclaimed, 'I would then redeem the promise which I made to you that evening, in the lane – outside Dover. Do you remember?'

She saw him stooping before her, and kissing her fingertips, even whilst her ears recalled every word he had spoken and every inflexion of his mocking voice:

'Let me rather put it differently, dear lady,' he had said then. 'One day the exquisite Theresia Cabarrus, the Egeria of the Terrorists, the fiancée of the great Tallien, might need the help of the Scarlet Pimpernel.'

And she, angered, piqued by his coolness, thirsting for revenge for the insult which she believed he had put upon her, had then protested earnestly:

'I would sooner die,' she had boldly asserted, 'than seek your help, milord!'

And now, at this hour, here in this house where Death lurked in every corner, she could still hear his retort:

'Here in Dover, perhaps . . . But in France?'

'You mean,' she had said at parting, 'that you would risk your life to save mine?'

'I should not risk my life, dear lady,' he had said with his puzzling smile; 'but I should – God help me! – do my best, if the need arose, to save yours.'

'You are bold, milord,' she said. 'And you are brave. Alas! what can you do, when the most powerful hands in France are against you?'

'Smite them, dear lady,' he replied airily. 'Smite them! Then turn my back upon this fair land. It will no longer have need of me.' Then he made her a courteous bow. 'May I have the honour of escorting you upstairs? Your friend M. Chauvelin will be awaiting you.'

His foot was on the step, ready to ascend, even whilst Theresia's straining ears caught the sound of other footsteps up above: footsteps of men – real men, those! – who were set up there to watch for the coming of the Scarlet Pimpernel, and whose vigilance had been spurred by promise of reward and by threat of death. She pushed his arm aside almost roughly.

'You are mad, milord!' she said, in a choked murmur. 'Such foolhardiness, when your life is in deadly jeopardy, becomes criminal folly –'

'The best of life,' he said airily, 'is folly. I would not miss this moment for a kingdom!'

She felt like a creature under a spell. He took her hand and drew it through his arm. She went up the steps beside him. Every moment she thought that one or more of the soldiers would be coming down, or that Chauvelin, impatient at her absence, might step out upon the landing.

On the landing he took leave of her, stooped and kissed her hand.

'Milord,' she entreated, 'on my knees I beg of you not to toy with your life any longer.'

'Toy with my life?' he retorted gaily. 'Nothing is further from my thoughts.'

'You must know that every second which you spend in this house is fraught with the greatest possible danger.'

'Danger? Ne'er a bit, dear lady! I am no longer in danger, now that you are my friend.'

The next moment he was gone. For a while, Theresia's straining ears still caught the sound of his firm footfall upon the stone steps. Then all was still; and she was left wondering if, in very truth, the last few minutes on the dark stairs had not all been part of a dream.

27 | *Terror or ambition*

CHAUVELIN had sufficiently recovered from the emotions of the past half-hour to speak coolly and naturally to Theresia. Whether he knew that she had waylaid Sir Percy Blakeney on the stairs or no, she could not conjecture. He made no reference to his interview with the Scarlet Pimpernel, nor did he question her directly as to whether she had overheard what passed between them.

'Vigilance!' he said to Theresia, after a curt greeting. 'Incessant vigilance, night and day, is what your country demands of you now, citizeness! All our lives now depend upon our vigilance.'

'Yours perhaps, citizen,' she rejoined coolly. 'You seem to forget that I am not bound –'

'You? Not bound?' he broke in roughly, and with a strident

laugh. 'Not bound to aid in bringing the most bitter enemy of your country to his knees? Not bound, now that success is in sight?'

'You only obtained my help by a subterfuge,' she retorted; 'by a forged letter and a villainous lie –'

'Bah! Are you going to tell me, citizeness, that all means are not justifiable when dealing with those whose hands are raised against France? Forgery?' he went on, with passionate earnestness. 'Why not? Outrage? Murder? I would commit every crime in order to serve the country which I love, and hound her enemies to death.'

He paused, carried away by his own enthusiasm, feeling perhaps that he had gone too far, or else had said enough to enforce the obedience which he exacted. After a while, since Theresia remained silent too, he added more quietly:

'If we capture the Scarlet Pimpernel this time, citizeness, Robespierre shall know from my lips that it is to you and to you alone that he owes this triumph over the enemy whom he fears above all. Without you, I could not have set the trap out of which he cannot now escape.'

'He can escape! He can!' she retorted defiantly. 'The Scarlet Pimpernel is too clever, too astute, too audacious, to fall into your trap.'

'Take care, citoyenne, take care! Your admiration for that elusive hero carries you beyond the bounds of prudence.'

'Bah! If he escapes, 'tis you who will be blamed –'

'And 'tis you who will suffer, citoyenne,' he riposted blandly. With which parting shaft he left her, certain that she would ponder over his threats as well as over his bold promise of a rich reward.

Theresia shuddered. Overhead she could hear the soldiers moving about, and in one of the rooms close by her sensitive ear caught the sound of Mother Théot's shuffling tread.

Impatient to get away from this atmosphere of tragedy which

was preying on her nerves, Theresia called to Mother Théot, and when the old woman came shuffling out of her room, demanded her cloak and hood.

'Have you seen aught of citizen Moncrif?' she asked, just before going away.

'I caught sight of him over the way,' Catherine Théot replied, 'watching this house, as he always does when you, citoyenne, are in it.'

'Ah!' the imperious beauty retorted, with a thought of spite in her mellow voice. 'Would you could give him a potion, Mother, to cure him of his infatuation for me!'

'Despise no man's love, citoyenne,' the witch retorted sententiously. 'Even that poor vagabond's blind passion may yet prove thy salvation.'

Down below, Bertrand Moncrif was waiting for her, silent, humble, with the look of a faithful watchdog upon his pale, wan face.

'You make yourself ill, my poor Bertrand,' Theresia said, not unkindly, seeing that he stood aside to let her pass, fearful of a rebuff if he dared speak to her. 'I am in no danger, I assure you; and this constant dogging of my footsteps can do no good to you or to me.'

'But it can do no harm,' he pleaded earnestly. 'Something tells me, Theresia, that danger does threaten you, unbeknown to you, from a quarter least expected.'

'Bah!' she retorted lightly. 'And, if it did, you could not avert it.'

Miserable Bertrand! He had laden his soul with an abominable crime for this woman's sake; and he had not even the satisfaction of feeling that she gave him an infinitesimal measure of gratitude.

28 | *In the meanwhile*

CHAUVELIN, who, despite his many failures, was still one of the most conspicuous – since he was one of the most unscrupulous – members of the Committee of Public Safety, had not attended its sittings for some days.

Robespierre, the tyrant, the autocrat whose mere word swayed the multitude, remained silent and impenetrable, absent from every gathering. Everyone knew that this man, dictator in all but name, was meditating a titanic attack upon his enemies. His veiled threats, uttered during his rare appearances at the speaker's tribune, embraced even the most popular, the most prominent, amongst the representatives of the people. Everyone, in fact, who was likely to stand in his way when he was ready to snatch the supreme power.

The Committee of Public Safety – now re-named the Revolutionary Committee – strove to ingratiate itself with the potential dictator and to pose before the people as alone pure and incorruptible, blind in justice, inexorable where the safety of the Republic was concerned. Thus an abominable emulation of vengeance and of persecution went on between the Committee and Robespierre's party, wherein neither side could afford to give in, for fear of being accused of apathy and of moderation.

Chauvelin, for the most part, had kept out of the turmoil. He felt that in his hands lay the destiny of either party. His one thought was of the Scarlet Pimpernel and of his imminent capture, knowing that, with the most inveterate opponent of revolutionary excesses in his hands, he would within an hour be in a position to link his triumph with one or other of the parties – either with Robespierre and his herd of butchers, or with Tallien and the Moderates.

He, Chauvelin, the despised, the derided, whose name had become synonymous with Failure, would then with a word sweep those aside who had mocked him, hurl his enemies from their pedestals, and name at will the rulers of France. All within four days!

And of these, two had gone by.

For Marguerite Blakeney, these days had gone by like a nightmare. Two days ago she had received a message, a few lines hastily scribbled by an unknown hand, and brought to her by the old woman who waited upon her.

'I have seen him,' the message said. 'He is well and full of hope. I pray God for your deliverance and his, but help can only come by a miracle.'

The message was written in a feminine hand, with no clue as to the writer.

Since then, nothing.

Marguerite had not seen Chauvelin again. But every day at a given hour she was conscious of his presence outside her door. She heard his voice in the vestibule: there would be a word or two of command, the grounding of arms, then some whispered talking; and presently Chauvelin's stealthy footstep would slink up to her door. And Marguerite would remain still as a mouse that scents the presence of a cat, holding her breath, life almost at a standstill in this agony of expectation.

In the late afternoons the air would become insufferably hot, and Marguerite would throw open the window and sit beside it, her gaze fixed upon the horizon far away, her hands lying limp and moist upon her lap.

She would dream . . . only to wake up the next moment to hear the church clock of St. Antoine striking seven, and a minute or two later that ominous shuffling footstep outside her door, those whisperings, the grounding of arms, a burst of cruel laughter, which brought her from the dizzy heights of illusive happiness back to the hideous reality of her own horrible position, and of the deadly danger which lay in wait for her beloved.

29 | *The close of the second day*

SOON after seven o'clock that evening the storm which had threatened all day burst in its full fury. A raging gale tore at the dilapidated roofs of this squalid corner of the great city, and lashed the mud of the streets into miniature cascades.

Chauvelin, who had paid his daily visit to the Captain in charge of the prisoner in the Rue de la Planchette, was unable to proceed homewards. For the moment the street appeared impassable. Wrapped in his cloak, he decided to wait in the disused storage-room below until it became possible for an unfortunate pedestrian to sally forth into the open.

His nerves were stretched to breaking-point, not only by incessant vigilance, the obsession of the one idea, the one aim, but also by multifarious incidents which his overwrought imagination magnified into attempts to rob him of his prey.

He trusted no one – not Mother Théot, not the men upstairs, not Theresia: least of all Theresia. His intimates – and he had a very few of these – said of him at that time that, if he had his way, he would have had every tatterdemalion in the city branded, like Rateau, lest they were bribed or tempted into changing identities with the Scarlet Pimpernel.

It was impossible to keep the outer doors open, because the

rain beat in wildly on that side, and the place would have been in utter darkness but for an old grimy lanthorn which some prudent hand had set upon a barrel in the centre of the vast space, and which shed a feeble circle of light around. The latch of the wicket appeared to be broken, for the small door, driven by the wind, flapped backwards and forwards with irritating ceaselessness. At one time Chauvelin tried to improvise some means of fastening it, for the noise helped to exacerbate his nerves and, leaning out into the street in order to seize hold of the door, he saw the figure of a man, bent nearly double in the teeth of the gale, shuffling across the street from the direction of the Porte St. Antoine.

It was then nearly eight o'clock, and the light treacherous, but despite the veil of torrential rain which intervened between him and that shuffling figure, something in the gait, the stature, the stoop of the wide, bony shoulders, appeared unpleasantly familiar. The man's head and shoulders were wrapped in a tattered piece of sacking, which he held close to his chest. His arms were bare, as were his shins, and on his feet he had a pair of sabots stuffed with straw.

Midway across the street he paused, and a tearing fit of coughing seemed to render him momentarily helpless. Chauvelin's first instinct prompted him to run to the stairs and to call for assistance from Captain Boyer. Indeed, he was half-way up to the first floor when, looking down, he saw that the man had entered the place through the wicket-door. Still coughing and spluttering, he had divested himself of his piece of sacking and was crouching down against the barrel in the centre of the room and trying to warm his hands by holding them against the glass sides of the old lanthorn.

From where he stood, Chauvelin could see the dim outline of the man's profile, the chin ornamented with a three-days' growth of beard, the lank hair plastered above the pallid forehead, the huge bones coated with grime, that protruded through the rags that did duty for a shirt. The sleeves of this tattered garment hung away from the arm, displaying a fiery, inflamed weal, shaped like the letter 'M', that had recently been burned into the flesh with a branding iron.

The sight of that mark upon the vagabond's arm caused Chauvelin to pause a moment, then to come down the stairs again.

'Citizen Rateau!' he called.

Rateau appeared terrified, scared by the sudden apparition of the man who had inflicted the shameful punishment upon him.

'I seem to have scared you, my friend,' Chauvelin remarked dryly.

'I – I did not know,' Rateau stammered with a painful wheeze, 'that anyone was here . . . I came for shelter . . .'

'I am here for shelter, too,' Chauvelin rejoined, 'and did not see you enter.'

'Mother Théot allows me to sleep here,' Rateau went on mildly. 'I have had no work for two days . . . not since . . .' And he looked down ruefully upon his arm. 'People think I am an escaped felon,' he explained with snivelling timidity. 'And I have always lived just from hand to mouth. In my quartier, the concierge turned me out of my lodging. They keep asking me what I have done to be branded like a convict.'

Chauvelin laughed.

'Tell them you've been punished for serving the English spy,' he said.

'The Englishman paid me well, and I am very poor,' Rateau retorted meekly. 'I could serve the State now . . . if it would pay me well.'

'Indeed? How?'

'By telling you something, citizen, which you would like to know.'

'What is it?'

For a moment Rateau leaned forward, struck the ground with his fist.

'Am I to be paid this time?' he asked.

'If you speak the truth – yes.'

'How much?'

'That depends on what you tell me. And now, if you hold your tongue, I shall call to the citizen Captain upstairs and send you to jail.'

The coalheaver appeared to crouch yet further into himself.

'Citizen Tallien will send me to the guillotine,' he murmured.

'What has citizen Tallien to do with it?'

'He pays great attention to the citoyenne Cabarrus.'

'And it is about her?'

Rateau nodded.

'What is it?' Chauvelin reiterated harshly.

'She is playing you false, citizen,' Rateau murmured in a hoarse breath, and crawled like a long, bulky worm a little closer to the Terrorist.

'How?'

'She is in league with the Englishman.'

'How do you know?'

'I saw her here . . . two days ago . . . You remember, citizen . . . after you . . .'

'Yes, yes!' Chauvelin cried impatiently.

'Sergeant Chazot took me to the cavalry barracks . . . They gave me drink . . . and I don't remember much what happened. But when I was myself again, I know that my arm was very sore, and when I looked down I saw this awful mark on it . . . I was just outside the Arsenal then . . . How I got there I don't know . . . I suppose Sergeant Chazot brought me back.'

'Yes, yes!'

'I came in here . . . My head still felt very strange . . . and my arm felt like living fire. Then I heard voices . . . they came from the stairs . . . I looked about me, and saw them standing there . . .'

Rateau, leaning upon one arm, stretched out the other and pointed to the stairs. Chauvelin with a violent gesture, seized him by the wrist.

'Who?' he queried harshly. Who was standing there?'

'The Englishman and citoyenne Cabarrus,' Rateau replied.

'You are certain?'

'I heard them talking —'

'What did they say?'

'I do not know . . . But I saw the Englishman kiss the citoyenne's hand before they parted.'

'And what happened after that?'

'The citoyenne went to Mother Théot's apartment and the Englishman came down the stairs. I had just time to hide behind that pile of rubbish. He did not see me.'

Chauvelin uttered a savage curse of disappointment.

'Is that all?' he exclaimed.

'The State will pay me?' Rateau murmured vaguely.

'Not a sou!' Chauvelin retorted roughly. 'And if citizen Tallien hears this pretty tale . . .'

'I can swear to it?'

'Bah! Citoyenne Cabarrus will swear that you lied. 'Twill be her word against that of a mudlark!'

'Nay!' Rateau retorted. ''Twill be more than that.'

'What then?'

'Will you swear to protect me, citizen, if citizen Tallien —'

'Yes, yes, I'll protect you . . . And the guillotine has no time to trouble about such muck-worms as you!'

'Well, then, citizen,' Rateau went on in a hoarse murmur, 'if you will go to the citoyenne's lodgings in the Rue Villedot, I can show you where the Englishman hides the clothes wherewith he disguises himself . . . and the letters which he writes to the citoyenne when . . .'

He paused, obviously terrified at the awesome expression of the other man's face. For a moment or two there was silence in the great disused store-room. Then Chauvelin murmured between his teeth:

'If I thought that she . . .' But he did not complete the sentence, jumped to his feet and approached the big mass of rags and humanity that cowered in the gloom. 'Get up, citizen Rateau!' he commanded.

The asthmatic giant struggled to his knees. His wooden shoes had slipped off his feet. He groped for them, and with trembling hands contrived to put them on again.

'Get up!' Chauvelin reiterated with a snarl like an angry tiger. He took a small tablet and a leaden point from his pocket, and stooping towards the light he scribbled a few words, and then handed the tablet to Rateau.

'Take this over to the Commissary of the Section in the Place du Carrousel. Half a dozen men and a captain will be detailed to go with you to the lodgings of the citoyenne Cabarrus in the Rue Villedot. You will find me there. Go!'

Rateau's hand trembled visibly as he took the tablet. He was obviously terrified at what he had done. But Chauvelin paid no further heed to him. He had given him his orders, knowing well that they would be obeyed.

In the vestibule on the top floor Chauvelin called to Captain Boyer.

'Citizen Captain,' he said at the top of his voice, 'you remember that tomorrow eve is the end of the third day?'

'Pardi!' the Captain retorted gruffly. 'Is anything changed?' 'No.'

'Then, unless by the eve of the fourth day that cursed Englishman is not in our hands, my orders are the same.'

'Your orders are,' Chauvelin rejoined loudly, and pointed with grim intention at the door behind which he felt Marguerite Blakeney to be listening for every sound, 'unless the

English spy is in our hands on the evening of the fourth day, to shoot your prisoner.'

'It shall be done, citizen!' Captain Boyer gave reply.

Then he grinned maliciously, because from behind the closed door there had come a sound like a quickly smothered cry.

After which Chauvelin nodded to the Captain and once more descended the stairs. A few seconds later he went out of the house into the stormy night.

30 | *When the storm burst*

FORTUNATELY the storm only broke after the bulk of the audience was inside the theatre. The performance was timed to commence at seven, and a quarter of an hour before that time the citizens of Paris who had come to applaud citoyenne Vestris, citoyen Talma, and their colleagues, in Chénier's tragedy, *Henry VIII* were in their seats.

But little was heard of the storm which raged outside; only at times the patter of rain on the domed roof became unpleasantly apparent as an inharmonious accompaniment to the declamation of the actors.

It seemed as if the members of the Convention and those who sat upon the Revolutionary Committee, as well as the more prominent speakers in the various Clubs, had made a point of showing themselves to the public, gay, unconcerned, interested in the stage and in the audience, at this moment when every man's head was insecure upon his shoulders and no man knew whether on reaching home he would not find a posse of the National Guard waiting to convey him to the nearest prison.

In one of the proscenium boxes, citizeness Cabarrus attracted a great deal of attention. Dressed with almost ostentatious simplicity, she drew all eyes upon her by her merry, ringing laughter, the ripple of conversation which flowed almost incessantly from her lips, and the graceful gestures of her bare hands and arms as she toyed with a miniature fan.

Indeed, Theresia Cabarrus was unusually light-hearted tonight. Sitting during the first two acts of the tragedy in her box, in the company of citizen Tallien, she became the cynosure of all eyes, proud and happy when, during the third interval, she received the visit of Robespierre.

He only stayed with her a few moments, and kept himself concealed for the most part at the back of the box; but he had been seen to enter, and Theresia's exclamation, 'Ah, citizen Robespierre! What a pleasant surprise! 'Tis not often you grace the theatre with your presence!' had been heard all over the house.

Tonight, whenever the audience caught sight of him in the Cabarrus's box, a wild cheer rang out from gallery to pit of the house. Then Theresia would lean over to him and whisper insinuatingly:

'You can do anything with that crowd, citizen. You hold the people by the magnetism of your presence and of your voice. There is no height to which you cannot aspire.'

'The greater the height,' he murmured moodily, 'the dizzier the fall . . .'

' 'Tis on the summit you should gaze,' she retorted; 'not on the abyss below.'

'I prefer to gaze into the loveliest eyes in Paris,' he replied with a clumsy attempt at gallantry; 'and remain blind to the summits as well as to the depths.'

She tapped her daintily shod foot on the floor and gave an

impatient little sigh. It seemed as if at every turn of fortune she was confronted with pusillanimity and indecision. Tallien fawning on Robespierre; Robespierre afraid of Tallien; Chauvelin a prey to nerves. How different from them all was that cool, self-possessed Englishman with the easy good-humour and splendid self-assurance!

When, a moment or two later, Robespierre took leave of her and she was left for a while alone with her thoughts, Theresia no longer tried to brush away from her mental vision the picture on which her mind loved to dwell. The tall, magnificent figure; the lazy, laughing eyes; the slender hand that looked so firm and strong amidst the billows of exquisite lace.

The next moment she was rudely awakened from her dreams. The door of her box was torn open by a violent hand, and turning, she saw Bertrand Moncrif, hatless, with hair dishevelled, clothes dripping and mud-stained, and linen soaked through. She was only just in time to arrest with a peremptory gesture the cry which was obviously hovering on his lips.

Tallien jumped to his feet.

'What is it?' he demanded in a quick whisper.

'A perquisition,' Moncrif replied hurriedly, 'in the house of the citoyenne!'

'Impossible!' she broke in harshly.

'I come from there,' Moncrif murmured. 'I have seen . . . heard . . .'

'Come outside,' Theresia interjected. 'We cannot talk here.'

She led the way out, and Tallien and Moncrif followed.

The corridor fortunately was deserted.

'Now, tell me!' she commanded.

Bertrand passed his trembling hand through his soaking hair. He was shaking from head to foot and appeared to have run till now he could scarcely stand.

'Tell me!' Theresia reiterated impatiently.

Tallien stood by, half paralysed with terror. He did not question the younger man, but gazed on him with compelling, horror-filled eyes, as if he would wrench the words out of him before they reached his throat.

'I was in the Rue Villedot,' Moncrif stammered breathlessly at last, 'when the storm broke. I sought shelter under the portico of a house opposite the citoyenne's lodgings ... I was there a long time. Then the storm subsided ... Men in uniform came along ... They were soldiers of the National Guard ... I could see that, though the street was pitch dark ... They passed quite close to me ... They were talking of the citoyenne ... Then they crossed over to her lodgings ... I saw them enter the house ... I saw citizen Chauvelin in the doorway ... He chided them for being late ... There was a captain, and there were six soldiers, and that asthmatic coalheaver was with them.'

'What!' Theresia exclaimed. 'Rateau?'

'They went into the house,' Moncrif went on, his voice rasping through his parched throat. 'I followed at a little distance, to make quite sure before I came to warn you. Fortunately I knew where you were ...'

'You are sure they went up to my rooms?' Theresia broke in quickly.

'Yes. Two minutes later I saw a light in your apartment.'

She turned abruptly to Tallien.

'My cloak!' she commanded. 'I left it in the box.'

It was Bertrand who went back for the cloak and wrapped her in it. She did not appear in the least afraid, but her wrath was terrible to see, and boded ill to those who had dared provoke it. Indeed, Theresia, flushed with her recent triumph and with Robespierre's rare if clumsy gallantries still ringing in her ear, felt ready to dare anything, to brave anyone – even Chauvelin and his threats. She even succeeded in reassuring Tallien, ordered him to remain in the theatre, and to show himself to the public as utterly unconcerned.

Then she wrapped her cloak about her and, taking Bertrand's arm, she hurried out of the theatre.

31 | *Our Lady of Pity*

It was like an outraged divinity in the face of sacrilege that Theresia Cabarrus appeared in the antechamber of her apartment, ten minutes later.

Her rooms were full of men; sentries were at the door; the furniture was overturned, the upholstery ripped up, cupboard doors swung open; even her bed and bedding lay in a tangled heap upon the floor. In the bedroom the maid Pepita, guarded by a soldier, was loudly lamenting in voluble Spanish. Citizen Chauvelin was standing in the centre of the living-room intent on examining some papers. In a corner of the antechamber cowered the ungainly figure of Rateau the coalheaver.

Theresia swept past the soldiers in the antechamber and confronted Chauvelin before he had time to notice her approach.

'Something has turned your brain, citizen Chauvelin,' she said coolly. 'What is it?'

He looked up, encountered her furious glance, and at once made her a profound, ironical bow.

'How wise was our young friend there to tell you of our visit, citoyenne!' he said suavely.

And he looked in mild approval in the direction where Bertrand Moncrif stood between two soldiers, who had quickly barred his progress and were holding him tightly by the wrists.

'I came,' Theresia retorted harshly, 'as the forerunner of those who will know how to punish this outrage, citizen Chauvelin.'

Once more he bowed, smiling blandly.

'I shall be as ready to receive them,' he said quietly, 'as I am gratified to see the citoyenne Cabarrus. When they come, shall I direct them to call and see their beautiful Egeria at the Conciergerie, whither we shall have the honour to convey her immediately?'

Theresia threw back her head and laughed; but her voice sounded hard and forced.

'On what charge, I pray you?' she demanded.

'Of trafficking with the enemies of the Republic.'

'You are mad, citizen Chauvelin!' she replied with perfect sang-froid. 'I pray you, order your men to re-establish order in my apartment; and remember that I will hold you responsible for any damage that has been done.'

'Shall I also,' Chauvelin rejoined, 'replace these letters and other interesting objects, there where we found them?'

'Letters?' she retorted, frowning. 'What letters?'

'These, citoyenne,' he replied, and held up to her gaze the papers which he had in his hand.

'What are they? I have never seen them before.'

'Nevertheless, we found them in that bureau.' And Chauvelin pointed to a small piece of furniture which stood against the wall, and the drawers of which had obviously been forcibly torn apart. Then as Theresia remained silent, he went on suavely: 'They are letters written at different times to Mme. de Fontenay, née Cabarrus – *Our Lady of Pity*, as she was called by grateful Bordeaux.'

'By whom?' she asked.

'By the interesting hero of romance who is known to the world as the Scarlet Pimpernel.'

'It is false!' she retorted firmly. 'I have never received a letter from him in my life!'

'His handwriting is all too familiar to me, citoyenne; and the letters are addressed to you.'

'It is false!' she reiterated with unabated firmness. 'You are mad, citizen Chauvelin! If there were letters writ by the Scarlet Pimpernel in my rooms, 'tis you who put them there! I repeat, 'tis you who put them there.'

"That statement you will be at liberty to substantiate to-morrow, citoyenne,' he retorted coldly, 'at the bar of the revolutionary tribunal. There, no doubt, you can explain away how citizen Rateau knew of the existence of those letters, and led me straight to their discovery. I have an officer of the National Guard, the commissary of the section, and half a dozen men, to prove the truth of what I say, and to add that in a wall-cupboard in your antechamber we also found this interesting collection, the use of which you, citoyenne, will no doubt be able to explain.'

He stepped aside and pointed to a curious heap which littered the floor – rags for the most part: a tattered shirt, frayed breeches, a grimy cap, a wig made up of lank, colourless hair, the counterpart of that which adorned the head of the coal-heaver Rateau.

Theresia looked on those rags for a moment in a kind of horrified puzzlement. She tried to laugh, to speak defiant words; but her throat felt as if it were held in a vice, and losing momentary consciousness she tottered, and only saved herself from measuring her length upon the floor by clinging with both hands to a table immediately behind her.

Chauvelin gave a curt word of command, and a couple of soldiers came and stood to right and left of her. Then a piercing cry rang through the narrow rooms, and she saw Bertrand Moncrif for one moment between herself and the soldiers, fighting desperately, shielding her with his body, tearing and raging like a wild animal defending its young. The whole room appeared full of a deafening noise: cries and more cries – words

T—F

of command – calls of rage and of entreaty. Then suddenly the
word 'Fire!' and the detonation of a pistol at close range, and
the body of Bertrand Moncrif sliding down limp and impotent
to the floor.

A thin, dry laugh brought her back to her senses, her pride
to the fore, her vanity up in arms. She drew her splendid figure
up to its full height and once more confronted Chauvelin.

'And at whose word,' she demanded, 'is this monstrous
charge to be brought against me?'

'At the word of a free citizen of the State,' Chauvelin replied
coldly.

'Bring him before me.'

Chauvelin shrugged his shoulders and smiled indulgently,
like one who is ready to humour a wayward child.

'Citizen Rateau!' he called.

From the anteroom there came the sound of much shuffling,
spluttering, and wheezing; then the dull clatter of wooden
shoes upon the carpeted floor; and presently the ungainly
grime-covered figure of the coalheaver appeared in the doorway.

Theresia looked on him for a few seconds in silence, then
she gave a ringing laugh, and with exquisite bare arm outstretched she pointed to the scrubby apparition.

'That man's word against mine!' she called, with well-
assumed mockery. 'Rateau the caitiff against Theresia Cabarrus,
the intimate friend of citizen Robespierre! In truth, citizen
Chauvelin, your spite must be hard put to it to bring up such
a witness against me!'

Then suddenly her glance fell upon the lifeless body of
Bertrand Moncrif, and on the horrible crimson stain which dis-
coloured his coat. She gave a shudder of horror, and for a
moment her eyes closed and her head fell back, as if she were
about to swoon. But she quickly recovered herself. She looked
with unutterable contempt on Chauvelin; then she raised her

cloak, and wrapped it with a queen-like gesture around her, and without another word led the way out of the apartment.

Chauvelin remained standing in the middle of the room, his face quite expressionless, his clawlike hands still fingering the fateful letters. Two soldiers remained with him beside the body of Bertrand Moncrif. The maid Pepita, still shrieking and gesticulating violently, had to be dragged away in the wake of her mistress.

In the doorway between the living-room and the ante-chamber, Rateau, humble, snivelling, more than a little fright-ened, stood aside in order to allow the guard and their im-perious prisoner to pass.

It was still raining hard. The captain who was in charge of Theresia told her that he had a chaise ready for her. Theresia ordered him to send for it; she would not, she said, offer herself as a spectacle to the riff-raff who happened to be passing by. The captain probably received orders to humour the prisoner as far as was compatible with safety. Certain it is that he sent one of his men to fetch the coach and to order the concierge to throw open the porte-cochère.

Theresia remained standing in the narrow vestibule at the foot of the stairs. Two soldiers stood on guard over the maid, whilst another stood beside Theresia. Rateau had paused on the stairs, a step or two just above where Theresia was standing. On the wall opposite, supported by an iron bracket, a smoky oil lamp shed a feeble, yellowish flicker around.

A few minutes went by; then a loud clatter woke the echoes of the dreary old house, and a coach lumbered into the court-yard and came to a halt in front of the open doorway. The captain gave a sigh of relief, and called out: 'Now then, citoyenne!' whilst the soldier who had gone to fetch the coach jumped down from the box-seat and, with his comrades, stood at attention. The maid was summarily bundled into the coach, and Theresia was ready to follow.

Just then the draught through the open door blew her velvet cloak against the filthy rags of the miserable ruffian behind her. An unexplainable impulse caused her to look up, and she encountered his eyes fixed upon her. A dull cry rose to her throat, and instinctively she put up her hand to her mouth, striving to smother the sound. Horror dilated her eyes, and through her lips one word escaped like a hoarse murmur:

'You!'

He put a grimy finger to his lips. But already she had recovered herself. Here then was the explanation of the mystery which surrounded this monstrous denunciation. The English milord had planned it as a revenge for the injury done to his wife.

'Captain!' she cried out shrilly. 'Beware! The English spy is at your heels!'

But apparently the captain's complaisance did not go to the length of listening to the ravings of his fair prisoner. He was impatient to get this unpleasant business over.

'Now then, citoyenne,' was his gruff retort. 'En voiture!'

'You fool!' she cried, bracing herself against the grip of the soldiers who were on the point of seizing her. ' 'Tis the Scarlet Pimpernel! If you let him escape –'

'The Scarlet Pimpernel?' the Captain retorted with a laugh. 'Where?'

'The coalheaver! Rateau! 'Tis he, I tell you.' And Theresia's cries became more frantic as she felt herself unceremoniously lifted off the ground. 'You fool You fool! You are letting him escape!'

'Rateau, the coalheaver?' the captain exclaimed. 'We have heard that pretty story before. Here, citizen Rateau!' he went on, and shouted at the top of his voice. 'Go and report yourself to citizen Chauvelin. Tell him you are the Scarlet Pimpernel! As for you, citoyenne, enough of this shouting – what? My orders are to take you to the Conciergerie, and not to run after spies – English, German, or Dutch. Now then, citizen soldiers! . . .'

She was ignominiously lifted into the coach and deposited by the side of equally noisy Pepita.

A moment of two later, Chauvelin, followed by the two soldiers, came quickly down the stairs. The noise from below had at last reached his ears. At first he too thought that it was only the proud Spaniard who was throwing her dignity to the winds. Then a word or two sounded clearly above the din:

'The Scarlet Pimpernel! The English spy!'

In an instant the rest of the world ceased to have any importance in his sight. One thing and one alone mattered; his enemy.

Calling to the soldiers to follow him, he was out of the apartment and down in the vestibule below in a trice. The coach at that moment was turning out of the porte-cochère. It was raining fast, and from the balconies the water was pouring down in torrents.

Chauvelin stood in the doorway and sent one of the soldiers to ascertain what the disturbance had all been about. The man returned with an account of how the aristo had screamed and raved like a madwoman, and tried to escape by sending the citizen captain on a fool's errand, vowing that poor Rateau was an English spy in disguise.

Chauvelin gave a sigh of relief. He certainly need not rack his nerves or break his head over that! He had good cause to know that Rateau, with the branded arm, could not possibly be the Scarlet Pimpernel!

32 | *Grey dawn*

TEN minutes later the courtyard and approach of the old house in the Rue Villedot were once more wrapped in silence and in darkness. Chauvelin had with his own hands affixed the official seals on the doors which led to the apartments of citoyenne Cabarrus. In the living-room, the body of the unfortunate Moncrif still lay uncovered and unwatched, awaiting what hasty burial the commissary of the section would be pleased to order for it. Chauvelin dismissed the soldiers at the door, and himself went his way.

The storm was gradually dying away. By the time that the audience filed out of the theatre, it was scarcely raining. Citizen Tallien hurried along on foot to the Rue Villedot. The last hour had been positive torture for him. His Theresia in the hands of rough soldiery – dragged to prison – he himself unable to ascertain what had become of her – until he saw her at the bar of that awful tribunal, from which there was no issue save the guillotine!

And with this dread came unendurable, gnawing remorse. He himself was one of the men who had helped to set up the machinery of wild accusations, monstrous tribunals and whole-sale condemnations which had been set in motion now by an unknown hand against the woman he loved.

He turned into the Rue Villedot. A minute or so later, he was making his way up the back staircase of the dingy house. On the second-floor landing two women stood gossiping. One of them recognized the influential Representative.

'It is citizen Tallien,' she said.

And the other woman at once volunteered the information:

166

They have arrested the citoyenne Cabarrus,' she said; 'and the soldiers did not know whither they were taking her.'

Tallien did not wait to listen further. He stumbled up the stairs to the third floor, to the door which he knew so well. His trembling fingers wandered over the painted panels. They encountered the official seals, which told their own mute tale.

The whole thing, then, was not a dream. Those assassins had taken his Theresia and dragged her to prison, would drag her on the morrow to an outrageous mockery of a tribunal first, and then to death!

For hours citizen Tallien sat in the dark, on the staircase outside Theresia's door, his head buried in his hands. The grey dawn, livid and chill, which came peeping in through the skylight overhead, found him still sitting there, stiff and numb with cold.

Then he heard – or thought he heard – firm, swift steps, and soon after saw the figures of two men coming up the stairs. Both men were very tall, one of them unusually so, and the ghostly light of dawn made him appear unreal and mysterious. Both the men wore huge coats of fine cloth, adorned with many capes, and boots of fine leather, perfectly cut.

They paused on the vestibule outside the door of Theresia's apartment, and appeared to be studying the official seals affixed upon the door. Then one of them – the taller of the two – took a knife out of his pocket and cut through the tapes which held the seals together. Then together they stepped coolly into the apartment.

Tallien watched them, dazed and fascinated. He was so numb and weary that his tongue – just as it does in dreams – refused him service when he tried to call. But now he struggled to his feet and followed in the wake of the two mysterious strangers. It did not occur to him to call for help. Somehow, the whole incident – the two men – were so ghostlike, that he felt that at a word they would vanish into thin air.

He stepped cautiously into the familiar little antechamber.
The strangers had gone through to the living-room. One of
them was kneeling on the floor. Tallien, who knew nothing
of the tragedy which had been enacted inside the apartment,
marvelled at what the men were doing. He crept stealthily forward and craned his neck to see. The window at the end of
the room had been left unfastened. A weird grey streak of
light came peeping in and illumined the awesome scene: the
overturned furniture, the torn hangings; and on the ground,
the body of a man, with the stranger kneeling beside it.

He could just see the tall stranger pass his hands over the body
on the floor, and could hear the other ask him a question in
English.

The strangers conversed in a low tone of voice. The taller
man of the two appeared to be giving his friend some orders,
which the latter promised to obey. Then, with utmost precaution, he took the body in his arms and lifted it from the
floor.

'Let me help you, Blakeney,' the other said in a whisper.

'No, no!' the mysterious stranger replied quickly. 'The poor
worm is as light as a feather!'

'Poor little Régine!' the younger man sighed.

'It is better so,' his friend rejoined. 'We'll be able to tell her
that he died nobly, and that we've given him a Christian burial.'

No wonder that Tallien thought that he was dreaming!
These English were strange folk indeed! Heaven alone knew
what they risked by coming here, at this hour, and into this
house, in order to fetch away the body of their friend.

Tallien held his breath. He saw the splendid figure of the
mysterious adventurer step across the threshold, bearing the
lifeless body in his arms with as much ease as if he were carrying a child. His friend came immediately behind him.

In the dark antechamber he paused, and called abruptly:
'Citizen Tallien!'

A cry rose to Tallien's throat. He had thought himself entirely unobserved, and the stranger a mere vision which he was watching in a dream.

But the spell was still on him, and he only moved in order to straighten himself out and to force his trembling knees to be still.

'They have taken the citoyenne Cabarrus to the Conciergerie,' the stranger went on simply. 'Tomorrow she will be charged before the Revolutionary Tribunal ... You know what is the inevitable end –'

It seemed as if some subtle magic was in the man's voice, in his very presence, in the glance wherewith he challenged that of the unfortunate Tallien. The latter felt a wave of shame sweep over him. There was something so splendid in these two men who rose braving and daring death in order to give Christian burial to their friend; whilst he, in face of the outrage put upon his beloved, had only sat on her desecrated doorstep like a dumb animal pining for its master. With quick, nervy movements he readjusted the set of his coat, passed his thin hands over his rumpled hair; whilst the stranger reiterated with solemn significance:

'You know what is the inevitable end ... The citoyenne Cabarrus will be condemned ...'

Tallien this time met the stranger's eyes fearlessly. It was the magic of strength and of courage that flowed into him from them.

'Not while I live!' he said firmly.

'Theresia Cabarrus will be condemned tomorrow, the stranger went on calmly. 'Then the next day, the guillotine –'

'Never!'

'Inevitably! ... Unless –'

'Unless what?' Tallient queried.

'Theresia Cabarrus, or Robespierre and his herd of assassins. Which shall it be, citizen Tallien?'

'By Heaven! –' Tallien exclaimed forcefully.

But he got no further. The stranger, bearing his burden, had already gone out of the room, closely followed by his friend.

Tallien rose, and strode with a firm step out of the apartment, carefully closing the doors behind him.

33 | *The cataclysm*

FORTY names! Found on a list in the pocket of Robespierre's coat!

Forty names! And every one of these that of a known opponent of Robespierre's schemes of dictatorship: Tallien, Barrère, Vadier, Cambon, and the rest. Men powerful today, prominent Members of the Convention, leaders of the people, too – but opponents!

The inference was obvious, the panic general. That night – it was the 8th Thermidor, July the 26th of the old calendar – men talked of flight, of abject surrender, of appeal – save the mark! – to friendship, camaraderie, humanity! They talked of everything, in fact, save of defying the tyrant; for such talk would have been folly.

So men talked and trembled. But Tallien, their chief, was nowhere to be found. 'Twas known that his fiancée, the beautiful Theresia Cabarrus, had been summarily arrested. Since then he had disappeared; and they – the others – were leaderless.

Robespierre then is to be dictator of France. He *will* be dictator of France! He has not said it; but his friends have shouted it from the house-tops, and have murmured under their breath that those who oppose Robespierre's dictatorship are traitors to the land. Death then must be their fate.

Behold the picture! A medley. A confusion. A whirl of everything that is passionate and cruel, defiant and desperate. Men who have thrown lives away as if lives were in truth grains of sand; men who have juggled with death, dealt it and tossed it about like cards upon a gaming table. They are desperate now, because their own lives are at stake; and they find now that life can be very dear.

So, having greeted their leader, the forty draw together, watching the moment when humility will be most opportune.

Robespierre mounts the tribune. The hour has struck. His speech is one long, impassioned, involved tirade, full at first of vague accusations against the enemies of the Republic and the people, and is full of protestations of his own patriotism and selflessness. Then he warms to his own oratory; his words are prophetic of death, his voice becomes harsh – like a screech owl's, so we're told. His accusations are no longer vague. He begins to strike.

Every victim spared from the guillotine is a traitor let loose against the people! A traitor, he who robs the guillotine of her prey! Robespierre stands alone incorruptible, true, faithful unto death! And for all that treachery, what remedy is there? The guillotine! New power to the sovereign guillotine! Death to all the traitors!

And seven hundred faces become paler still with dread, and the sweat of terror rises on seven hundred brows. There were only forty names on that list . . . but there might be others somewhere else!

And still the voice of Robespierre thunders on. His words fall on seven hundred pairs of ears as on a sounding-board; his friends, his sycophants, echo them; they applaud, rise in wild enthusiasm.

One of the tyrant's most abject slaves has put forward the motion that the great speech just delivered shall forthwith be printed, and distributed to every township, every village, throughout France, as a monument to the lofty patriotism of her greatest citizen. The motion at one moment looks as if it would be carried with acclamations; after which, Robespierre's triumph would have risen to the height of deification. Then suddenly the note of dissension; the hush; the silence. Something has turned the acclamations to mutterings, and then to silence. Citizen Tallien has demanded 'delay in printing that speech,' and asked pertinently:

'What has become of the Liberty of Opinion in this Convention?'

There is a flutter in the Convention, a moment's hesitation. But the question *is* put to the vote, and the speech is *not* to be printed.

Robespierre, lofty in his scorn, puts the notes of his speech into his pocket. He does not condescend to argue. He, the master of France, will not deign to bandy words with his slaves. And he stalks out of the Hall surrounded by his friends.

His withdrawal – proud, silent, menacing – is in keeping with his character and with the pose which he has assumed of late. But he is still the Chosen of the People; and the multitude is there, thronging the streets of Paris – there, to avenge the insult put upon their idol by a pack of slinking wolves.

And now the picture becomes still more poignant. The morning breaks on the 9th Thermidor, and again the Hall of Convention is crowded to the roof, with Tallien and his friends, in a close phalanx, early at their post!

Tallien is there, pale, resolute, the fire of his hatred kept up by anxiety for his beloved. The night before, at the corner of a dark street, a hand slipped a scrap of paper into the pocket of his coat. It was a message written with her own blood. How it ever came into his pocket Tallien never knew; but the few impassioned, agonized words seared his very soul and whipped up his courage:

'The Commissary of Police has just left me,' Theresia wrote. 'He came to tell me that tomorrow I must appear before the tribunal. This means the guillotine. And I, who thought that you were a *man* . . . !'

St. Just on this occasion is the first to mount the tribune; and Robespierre stands silently by. He has spent the afternoon and evening with his friends at the Jacobins' Club, where deafening applause greeted his every word, and wild fury raged against his enemies. No sooner has St. Just mounted the tribune than Tallien jumps to his feet. His voice, usually meek and cultured, rises in a harsh crescendo, until it drowns that of the younger orator.

'Citizens,' he exclaims, 'I ask for truth! Let us tear aside the curtain behind which lurk concealed the real conspirators and the traitors!'

'Yes, yes! Truth! Let us have the truth!' One hundred voices – not forty – have raised the echo.

The mutiny is on the verge of becoming open revolt, is that already, perhaps. It is like a spark fallen – who knows where? – into a powder magazine. Robespierre feels it, sees the spark. He rushes to the tribune, tries to mount. But Tallien has forestalled him, elbows him out of the way, and turns to the seven hundred with a cry that rings far beyond the Hall, out into the streets.

'Citizens!' he thunders in his turn. 'I begged of you just now to tear aside the curtains behind which lurk the traitors. Well, the curtain is already rent. And if you dare not strike at the tyrant now, then 'tis I who will dare!' And from beneath his coat he draws a dagger and raises it above his head. 'And I will plunge this into his heart,' he cries, 'if you have not the courage to smite!'

His words, that gleaming bit of steel, fan the spark into a

flame. Within a few seconds, seven hundred voices are shouting, 'Down with the tyrant!'

At this hour all is confusion and deafening uproar. In vain Robespierre tries to speak. He demands to speak. He hurls insults, anathema, upon the President, who relentlessly refuses him speech and jingles his bell against him.

'President of Assassins,' the falling tyrant cries, 'I demand speech of thee!'

But the bell goes jingling on, and Robespierre, choked with rage and terror, 'turns blue' we are told, and his hand goes up to his throat.

'The blood of Danton chokes thee!' cries one man. And these words seem like the last blow dealt to the fallen foe. The next moment the voice of an obscure Deputy is raised, in order to speak the words that have been hovering on every lip:

'I demand a decree of accusation against Robespierre!'

'Accusation!' comes from seven hundred throats. 'The decree of accusation!'

The President jingles his bell, puts the question, and the motion is passed unanimously.

Maximilien Robespierre – erstwhile master of France – is decreed *accused*.

34 | *The whirlwind*

IT was then noon. Five minutes later, the Chosen of the People, the fallen idol, is hustled out of the hall into one of the Committee rooms close by, and with his friends – St. Just, Couthon, Lebas, his brother Augustin, and the others – all decreed accused and the order of arrest launched against them. As for the rest, 'tis the work of the Public Prosecutor – and of the guillotine.

At five o'clock the Convention adjourns. The deputies rush to their homes, there to relate what has happened; Tallien to the Conciergerie, to get a sight of Theresia. This is denied him. He is not dictator yet; and Robespierre, though apparently vanquished, still dominates – and lives.

In the city all is hopeless confusion. Men are running in every direction, shouting, brandishing pistols and swords.

Proclamations are read at street corners; there are rumours of a general massacre of all the prisoners. At one moment – the usual hour – the familiar tumbril with its load of victims for the guillotine rattles along the cobble-stones of the Rue St. Antoine. The populace, vaguely conscious of something stupendous in the air – even though the decree of accusation against Robespierre has not yet transpired – loudly demand the release of the victims. They surround the tumbrils, crying, 'Let them be free!'

But Henriot at the head of his gendarmes comes riding down the street, and while the populace shouts, 'It shall not be! Let them be free!' he threatens with pistols and sabre, and retorts, bellowing: 'It shall be! To the guillotine!' And the tumbrils, which for a moment had halted, lumber on, on their way.

Up in the attic of the lonely house in the Rue de la Planchette, Marguerite Blakeney heard but a mere faint echo of the confusion and of the uproar.

But it was all very vague, for her nerves by this time were on the rack. She had lost count of time, of place; she knew nothing. All her instincts were merged in the dread of that silent evening hour, when Chauvelin's furtive footsteps would once more resound upon the stone floor outside her door, when she would hear the quick word of command that heralded his approach, the grounding of arms, the sharp query and quick answer, and when she would feel again the presence of the relentless enemy who lay in wait to trap her beloved.

At one moment that evening he had raised his voice, obviously so that she might hear.

'Tomorrow is the fourth day, citizen Captain,' she heard him say. 'I may not be able to come.'

'Then,' the voice of the Captain had said in reply, 'if the Englishman is not here by seven o'clock –'

Chauvelin had given a harsh, dry laugh, and retorted:

'Your orders are as they were, citizen. But I think that the Englishman will come.'

What it all meant Marguerite could not fail to conjecture. It meant death to her or to her husband – to both, in fact. And all today she had sat by the open window, her hands clasped in silent, constant prayer, her eyes fixed upon the horizon far away, longing with all her might for one last sight of her beloved, fighting against despair, striving for trust in him and for hope.

At this hour, the centre of interest is the Place de l'Hôtel de Ville, where Robespierre and his friends sit entrenched and – for the moment – safe. The prisons have refused one by one to close their gates upon the Chosen of the People; governors and jailers alike have quaked in the face of so monstrous a sacrilege. And the same gendarmes who have been told off to escort the fallen tyrant, have had a touch of the same kind of scruple – or dread – and at his command have conveyed him to the Hôtel de Ville.

In vain does the Convention hastily reassemble. In vain – apparently – does Tallien demand that the traitor Robespierre and his friends be put outside the pale of the law. They are for the moment safe whilst Henriot and his gendarmes, having struck terror in the hearts of all peaceable citizens, hold the place outside the Town Hall and proclaim Robespierre dictator of France.

From time to time, troops of the Municipal gendarmes ride furiously by, with shouts of 'Robespierre! Robespierre! Death to the traitors! Long live Robespierre!'

As soon as they have gone by, excited groups close up in their wake. Gossip, conjectures, rumours, hold undisputed sway.

'Robespierre is dictator of France!'

'He has ordered the arrest of all the Members of the Convention.'

'And the massacre of all the prisoners.'

'Pardi, a wise decree! As for me, I am sick of the eternal tumbrils and the guillotine!'

And so, from mouth to mouth! The meek and the peace-loving magnify these rumours into approaching cataclysm; the opportunists hold their tongue, ready to fall in with this party or that; the cowards lie in hiding and shout 'Robespierre!' with Henriot's horde or 'Tallien!' in the neighbourhood of the Tuileries.

Here the Convention has reassembled, and here they are threatened by Henriot and his artillery. The members of the great Assembly remain at their post. The President has harangued them.

'Citizen deputies!' he calls aloud. 'The moment has come to die at our posts!'

And they sit waiting for Henriot's cannonade, and calmly decree all the rebels 'outside the pale of the law'.

Citizen Barras is promoted Commandant of the National Guard and of all forces at the disposal of the Convention, and ordered to recruit loyal troops that will stand up to the traitor Henriot and his ruffianly gendarmes. The latter are in open revolt against the Government; but, name of a name! Citizen Barras, with a few hundred patriots, will soon put reason – and a few charges of gunpowder – into them!

So, at five o'clock in the afternoon, whilst Henriot has once more collected his gendarmes and the remnants of his artillery outside the Hôtel de Ville, citizen Barras, accompanied by two aides-de-camp, goes forth on his recruiting mission. He makes the round of the city gates, wishing to find out what loyal soldiers amongst the National Guard the Convention can rely upon.

Chauvelin, on his way to the Rue de la Planchette, meets Barras at the Porte St. Antoine; and Barras is full of the news.

'Why were you not at your place at the Assembly, citizen Chauvelin?' he asks of his colleague. 'It was the grandest moment I have ever witnessed! Tallien was superb, and Robespierre ignoble! And if we succeed in crushing that bloodthirsty monster once and for all, it will be a new era of civilization and liberty!'

He halts, and continues with a fretful sigh:

'But we want soldiers – loyal soldiers! All the troops that we can get! Henriot has the whole of the Municipal Gendarmerie at his command, with muskets and guns; and Robespierre can always sway that rabble with a word. We want men! ... Men! ...'

But Chauvelin is in no mood to listen. Robespierre's fall or his triumph, what are they to him at this hour, when the curtain is about to fall on the final act of his own stupendous drama of revenge? Whatever happens, whoever remains in power, vengeance is his! The English spy in any event is sure of the guillotine.

So Chauvelin listens unmoved to Barras's passionate tirades, and when the latter, puzzled at his colleague's indifference, reiterates frowning:

'I must have all the troops I can get. You have some capable soldiers at your command always, citizen Chauvelin. Where are they now?'

Chauvelin retorts dryly:

'At work. On business at least as important as taking sides in a quarrel between Robespierre and Tallien.'

'Pardi! . . .' Barras protests hotly.

But Chauvelin pays no further attention to him. A neighbouring church clock has just struck six. Within the hour his arch enemy will be in his hands!

Chauvelin turns on his heel, and stumbles against a man who sits on the ground, with his back to the wall, munching a straw, his knees drawn up to his nose, a crimson cap pulled over his eyes, and his two long arms encircling his shins.

Chauvelin looked down, and saw the one long arm branded with the letter 'M', the flesh still swollen and purple with the fire of the searing iron.

'Rateau!' he ejaculated roughly. 'What are you doing here?'

Meek and servile, Rateau struggled with some difficulty to his feet.

'I have finished my work at Mother Théot's, citizen,' he said humbly. 'I was resting.'

Chauvelin kicked at him with the toe of his boot.

'Then go and rest elsewhere,' he muttered. 'The gates of the city are not refuges for vagabonds.'

After which act of unnecessary brutality he walked rapidly through the gate.

Barras had stood by during this brief interlude, vaguely interested in the little scene. But now, when the coalheaver lurched past him, one of his aides-de-camp remarked audibly:

'An unpleasant customer, citizen Chauvelin! Eh, friend?'

'I believe you!' Rateau replied readily enough. Then, with mulish persistence of a gaby who is smarting under a wrong, he thrust out his branded arm, right under citizen Barras's nose. 'See what he has done to me!'

Barras frowned.

'A convict, what? Then, how is it you are at large?'

'I am an innocent man, and a free citizen of the Republic. But I got in citizen Chauvelin's way, what? He is always full of schemes —'

'You are right there!' Barras retorted grimly.

'If you will but listen, citizen,' Rateau wheezed painfully, 'I can tell you —'

'What?'

'You were asking citizen Chauvelin where you could find some soldiers of the Republic to do you service.'

'Yes; I did.'

'Well,' Rateau rejoined, and an expression of malicious cunning distorted his ugly face. 'I can tell you.'

'What do you mean?'

'I lodge in an empty warehouse over yonder,' Rateau went on eagerly, and pointed in the direction where Chauvelin's spare figure had disappeared a while ago. 'The floor above is inhabited by Mother Théot, the witch. You know her, citizen?'

'Yes, yes! I thought she had been sent to the guillotine along with —'

'She was let out of prison, and has been doing some of citizen Chauvelin's spying for him.'

Barras frowned.

'To the point, citizen!' he said curtly.

'Citizen Chauvelin has a dozen or more soldiers under his command, in that house,' Rateau went on with a leer. 'They are trained troops of the National Guard –'

'How do you know?' Barras broke in harshly.

'Pardi!' was the coalheaver's dry reply. 'I clean their boots for them.'

'Where is the house?'

'In the Rue de la Planchette. But there is an entrance into the warehouse at the back of it.'

'Allons!' was Barras's curt word of command, to the two men who accompanied him.

He strode up the street towards the gate, not caring whether Rateau came along or no. But the coalheaver followed in the wake of the three men. He had buried his grimy fists once more in the pocket of his tattered breeches; but not before he had shaken them, each in turn, in the direction of the Rue de la Planchette.

Chauvelin in the meanwhile had turned into Mother Théot's house, and mounted to the top floor. Here he called peremptorily to Captain Boyer.

'There is half an hour yet,' the latter murmured gruffly; 'and I am sick of all this waiting! Let me finish with that cursed aristo in there. My comrades and I want to see what is going on in the city, and join in the fun, if there is any.'

'Half an hour, citizen,' Chauvelin rejoined dryly. 'You'll lose little of the fun, and you'll certainly lose your share of the ten thousand livres if you shoot the woman and fail to capture the Scarlet Pimpernel.'

'Bah! He'll not come now,' Boyer riposted. 'It is too late. He is looking after his own skin, pardi!'

'He will come I swear!' Chauvelin said firmly, as if in answer to his own thoughts.

A distant church clock strikes the half-hour . . . a short half-hour now . . .

Then suddenly Boyer, the Captain of the ruffians, exclaims loudly:

'Let me finish with the aristo, citizen Chauvelin! I want to join in the fun.'

And the door of her room is torn open by a savage, violent hand. The window behind Marguerite is open, and she, facing the door, clings with both hands to the sill. Her cheeks bloodless, her eyes glowing, her head erect, she waits, praying with all her might for courage . . . only courage.

The ruffianly captain, in his tattered, mud-stained uniform, stands in the doorway – for one moment only. The next, Chauvelin has elbowed him out of the way, and in his turn faces the prisoner – the innocent woman whom he has pursued with such relentless hatred.

Chauvelin speaks to her; she does not hear. There is a mighty buzzing in her ears as of men shouting – shouting what, she does not know, for she is still praying for courage. Chauvelin has ceased talking. Then it must be the end. Thank God! she has had the courage not to speak and not to flinch . . .

With closed eyes, Marguerite suddenly seems able to hear. She hears shouts which come from below – quite close, and coming nearer every moment. Shouts, and the tramp, the scurry of many feet; and now and then that wheezing, asthmatic cough, that strange, strange cough, and the click of wooden shoes. Then a voice, harsh and peremptory:

'Citizen soldiers, your country needs you! Rebels have defied her laws. To arms! Every man who hangs back is a deserter and a traitor!'

After this, Chauvelin's sharp, dictatorial voice raised in protest:

'In the name of the Republic, citizen Barras –'

But the other breaks in more peremptorily still:

'Ah, ça, citizen Chauvelin! Do you presume to stand between me and my duty? By order of the Convention now assembled, every soldier must report at once to his section. Are you perchance on the side of the rebels?'

At this point, Marguerite opens her eyes. Through the widely open door she sees the small, sable-clad figure of Chauvelin, his pale face distorted with rage to which he obviously dare not give rein; and beside him a short, stoutish man in cloth coat and cord breeches, and with the tricolour scarf around his waist. The two men appear to be defying one another; and all around them are the vague forms of the soldiers silhouetted against a distant window, through which the crimson afternoon glow comes peeping in on a cloud of flickering dust.

'Now then, citizen soldiers!' Barras resumes, and turns his back on Chauvelin, who, white to the lips, raises a final and menacing word of warning.

'I warn you, citizen Barras,' he says firmly, 'that, by taking these men away from their post, you place yourself in league with the enemy of your country, and will have to answer to her for this crime.'

His accent is so convinced, so firm, and fraught with such dire menace, that for one instant Barras hesitates.

'Eh bien!' he exclaims. 'I will humour you thus far, citizen Chauvelin. I will leave you a couple of men to wait on your pleasure until sundown. But, after that . . .'

For a second or two there is silence. Chauvelin stands there, with his thin lips pressed tightly together. Then Barras adds, with a shrug of his wide shoulders:

'I am contravening my duty in doing even so much; and the responsibility must rest with you, citizen Chauvelin. Allons, my men!' he says once more; and without another glance on his discomfited colleague, he strides down the stairs, followed by Captain Boyer and the soldiers.

For a while the house is still filled with confusion and

sounds: men tramping down the stone stairs, words of command, click of sabres and muskets, opening and slamming of doors. Then the sounds slowly die away, out in the street in the direction of the Porte St. Antoine.

Chauvelin stands in the doorway with his back to the room and to Marguerite, his claw-like hands intertwined convulsively behind him. The silhouette of the two remaining soldiers are still visible; they stand silently and at attention with their muskets in their hands. Between them and Chauvelin hovers the tall, ungainly figure of a man, clothed in rags and covered in soot and coal-dust. His feet are thrust into wooden shoes, his grimy hands are stretched out each side of him; and on his left arm, just above the wrist, there is an ugly mark like the brand seared into the flesh of a convict.

Chauvelin curtly bids him stand aside; and at the same moment the church clock of St. Louis, close by, strikes seven.

'Now then, citizen soldiers!' Chauvelin commands.

The soldiers grasp their muskets more firmly, and Chauvelin raises his hand. The next instant he is thrust violently back into the room, loses his balance, and falls backwards against a table, whilst the door is slammed to between him and the soldiers. From the other side of the door there comes the sound of a short, sharp scuffle. Then silence.

Chauvelin struggled painfully to his feet. With a mighty effort and a hoarse cry of rage, he threw himself against the door. The impetus carried him farther than he intended, no doubt; for at that same moment the door was opened, and he fell up against the massive form of the grimy coalheaver, whose long arms closed round him, lifted him off the floor, and carried him like a bundle of straw to the nearest chair.

'There, my dear M. Chambertin!' the coalheaver said, in exceedingly light and pleasant tones. 'Let me make you quite comfortable!'

Marguerite watched – dumb and fascinated – the dexterous

hands that twined a length of rope round the arms and legs of her helpless enemy, and wound his own tricolour scarf around that snarling mouth.

She scarcely dared trust her eyes and ears.

There was the hideous, dust-covered mudlark with bare feet thrust into sabots, with ragged breeches and tattered shirt; there was the cruel, mud-stained face, the purple lips, the toothless mouth; and those huge, muscular arms, one of them branded like the arm of a convict, the flesh still swollen with the searing of the iron.

'I must indeed crave your ladyship's forgiveness. In very truth, I am a disgusting object!'

Ah, there was the voice! – the dear, dear, merry voice!

'You did not doubt, m'dear, that I would come?' he asked quaintly.

She shook her head.

'Will you ever forgive me?' he continued.

'Forgive? What?' she murmured.

'These last few days. I could not come before. You were safe for the time being ... That fiend was waiting for me ...'

She gave a shudder and closed her eyes.

'Where is he?'

He laughed his gay, irresponsible laugh, and with a slender hand, still covered with coal-dust, he pointed to the helpless figure of Chauvelin.

'Look at him!' he said. 'Doth he not look a picture?'

Marguerite ventured to look. Even at sight of her enemy bound tightly with ropes to a chair, his own tricolour scarf wound loosely round his mouth, she could not altogether suppress a cry of horror.

'What is to become of him?'

He shrugged his broad shoulders.

'I wonder!' he said lightly.

Then he rose to his feet, and went on with quaint bashfulness:

'I wonder,' he said, 'how I dare stand thus before your ladyship!'

And in a moment she was in his arms, laughing, crying, covered herself now with coal-dust and with grime.

'My beloved!' she exclaimed with a shudder of horror. 'What you must have gone through!'

He only laughed like a schoolboy who has come through some impish adventure without much harm.

'Very little, I swear!' he asserted gaily. 'But for thoughts of you, I have never enjoyed anything so much as this last phase of a glorious adventure. After our clever friend here ordered the real Rateau to be branded, so that he might know him again wherever he saw him, I had to bribe the veterinary who had done the deed, to do the same thing for me. It was not difficult. For a thousand livres the man would have branded his own mother on the nose; and I appeared before him as a man of science, eager for an experiment. He asked no questions. And, since then, whenever Chauvelin gazed contentedly on my arm, I could have screamed for joy! I shall always love that scar, for the exciting time it recalls and because it happens to be the initial of your dear name.'

After which he had to tell her as quickly and as briefly as he could, all that had happened in the past few days.

'It was only by risking the fair Theresia's life,' he said, 'that I could save your own. No other spur would have goaded Tallien into open revolt.'

He turned and looked down for a moment on his enemy, who lay pinioned and helpless, with hatred and baffled revenge writ plainly on the contorted face and pale, rolling eyes.

And Sir Percy Blakeney sighed, a quaint sigh of regret.

'I only regret one thing, my dear M. Chambertin,' he said

after a while. 'And that is, that you and I will never measure wits again after this. Your damnable revolution is dead ... your unsavoury occupation gone ... I am glad I was never tempted to kill you. I might have succumbed, and in very truth robbed the guillotine of an interesting prey. Without any doubt, they will guillotine the lot of you, my good M. Chambertin. Robespierre tomorrow; then his friends, his sycophants, his imitators – you amongst the rest ... 'Tis a pity! You have so often amused me. Especially after you had put a brand on Rateau's arm, and thought you would always know him after that. Think it all out, my dear sir! Remember our happy conversation in the warehouse down below, and my denunciation of citoyenne Cabarrus ... You gazed upon my branded arm then and were quite satisfied. My denunciation was a false one, of course! 'Tis I who put the letters and the rags in the beautiful Theresia's apartments. But she will bear me no malice, I dare swear! for I shall have redeemed my promise. Tomorrow, after Robespierre's head has fallen, Tallien will be the greatest man in France and his Theresia a virtual queen. Think it all out, my dear Monsieur Chambertin! You have plenty of time. Someone is sure to drift up here presently, and will free you and the two soldiers, whom I left out on the landing. But no one will free you from the guillotine when the time comes, unless I myself ...'

He did not finish; the rest of the sentence was merged in a merry laugh.

'A pleasant conceit – what?' he said lightly. 'I'll think on it, I promise you!'

And the next day Paris went crazy with joy. Never had the streets looked more gay, more crowded. The windows were filled with spectators; the very roofs were crowded with an eager, shouting throng.

The seventeen hours of agony were ended. He, who yesterday was the Chosen of the People, the Messenger of the Most

High, now sat, or rather lay, in the tumbril, with broken jaw, eyes closed.

The end came at four in the afternoon, in the midst of acclamations from a populace drunk with gladness – acclamations which found their echo in the whole of France, and have never ceased to re-echo to this day.

But of all that tumult, Marguerite and her husband heard little. They lay snugly concealed the whole of that day in the quiet lodgings in the Rue de l'Anier, which Sir Percy had occupied during those terribly anxious times. Here they were waited on by that asthmatic reprobate Rateau and his mother, both of whom were now rich for the rest of their days.

When the shades of evening gathered in over the jubilant city, whilst the church bells were ringing and the cannons booming, a market gardener's cart, driven by a worthy farmer and his wife, rattled out of the Porte St. Antoine. It created no excitement, and suspicion was far from everybody's mind. The passports appeared in order; but even if they were not, who cared, on this day of all days, when tyranny was crushed and men dared to be men again?

These are other Knight Books

THE SCARLET PIMPERNEL

Baroness Orczy

In France the Revolution was at its height.
In England people danced and sang and went
about their ordinary life. But a small band of
brave men, under their leader the Scarlet
Pimpernel, were engaged in rescuing French
aristocrats from the very knife of the guillotine.
*The famous and popular historical romance which has
been translated into nearly every language in the world.*

THE LAND THE RAVENS FOUND

Naomi Mitchison

A story of the late viking age, and in particular
of Anlaf, the master now that his father has been
killed in battle. Threatened with death and
destruction, his little community builds a ship
and sails to Iceland – the land the ravens found.
Here they set about their new life: here they
meet the dangers and fears of this awesome
unfamiliar world.
Naomi Mitchison is the distinguished novelist,
critic and poet.

HOUNDS OF THE KING

Henry Treece

1066 – the field of what is now called
Hastings. The Hounds of the King, Harold's
personal warriors, gather for the last time to
protect their king against the Normans.
One of these warriors is Beornoth, and this
book is about his life in Harold's service.
It is a story of heroism and adventure, and a
magnificent picture of Saxon England.

THE HILLS OF VARNA

Geoffrey Trease

The year is 1509. A University brawl sends
Alan Drayton fugitive across Europe seeking
an ancient manuscript.
In Venice, at the house of Aldus Manutius,
the famous printer, he meets Angela. From
then on she shares his adventures: Adriatic
piracy, blood feuds, wild Turkish riders,
the sinister Monks of Varna. And always
in the shadows, stalks their arch-enemy and
rival, Cesare Morelli, crafty, clever and
unscrupulous.
*Acknowledged by many critics to be the best
and most exciting of all historical adventure
stories by this renowned novelist.*

Two books about life and riding on the Hungarian Plains, by *Kate Seredy*.

THE GOOD MASTER

The famous story about Uncle Marton and his family and his niece Kate, who comes to live with them.

THE SINGING TREE

It is wartime, and Uncle Marton goes away to fight, leaving his son Jancsi in charge of the ranch.

Both books are newly illustrated by the notable artist Imre Hofbauer who, like the author, was born in Hungary and knows well the life so finely presented here.